The first time we met was at a party.

Your ex arrived to show off the person he'd left you for last month, and you asked me to pretend to be your date. I was more than happy to help. You were attractive, smart, and witty—and that kiss we shared? It left me wanting you for days.

The second time we met was in my office on campus where we were both surprised to discover you were the new master's degree student in poetry I would be working with. You promised to be professional. I did no such thing.

The late nights and intense study sessions spent alongside you majorly throw me off my game. I want you, and I fight with myself daily over this fact.

I know I'm crass, that my sexual innuendos and dirty mouth annoy you, but I live for those two bright spots of color in your cheeks. If that's the only reaction I can get out of you, I'll gladly take it.

You hate Mondays, so every Monday I slip an anonymous poem into your bag and your smile gets me through the week.

I think I'm falling for you, and I know it's wrong. I know that I'm only supposed to be the adviser to your program and nothing more, but here's the thing. I think you're falling for me, too.

xo, Zach

Chapter One

Zach

"When was the last time you've been laid, son?"

Mom studied me over the rim of her reading spectacles with a knowing smirk.

Jesus.

I almost spit out my coffee. "Mom, we're not discussing that. Boundaries. Remember? We've talked about this."

My mother lacked a filter, and she seemed inordinately curious about the state of my sex life. I kept telling myself that was only because she didn't have one. *Please let that be the reason.*

She merely shrugged. "I worry, you know."

The truth was, the only thing that went down on me this weekend was my Wi-Fi.

But worse than that? My own fucking mother pointing out my dry spell to me in such vivid detail.

"I'm fine, Mom. Seriously. You don't need to worry."

I knew enough to know we probably didn't have a normal mother-son relationship. My parents had divorced when I was young, and I was raised primarily by my mother, and so we'd always been incredibly close.

"Zach, you don't have to be in a committed relationship to have intercourse," she paused to take a sip of her coffee, smiling again, "or so I've heard."

"I'm well aware of that," I gritted out. "Thanks, Mom."

Twice a week, my calendar was marked for a date at the same café with one of the sweetest, and nosiest women in town—you guessed it—my mother. This probably didn't help my limited social life outside of university events and the occasional evening out, but she was bored out of her mind after retiring, and since she lived not far from campus, it was a tradition we'd adopted. And one that I was quickly starting to rethink.

I must have gotten my early morning gene from her because she always managed to beat me here, so that she was primed and ready to fire off questions as soon as I arrived. Admittedly, my commute was a bit longer than hers. Working at the university, I learned damn quick which coffee shops and bars were far enough from campus to avoid running into students, and I was more than willing to drive across town to avoid a student hearing my mother discussing my sex life a little too loudly.

Mom leaned forward and patted the back of my hand. "So, what's really going on, sweetie? What's with the dry spell? Your aura is all out of whack." She swished her hand in the air in front of my face as if to wipe the bad vibes away.

"At least let me get some caffeine in my system before you cleanse my aura." I plastered on a fake smile.

After I'd taken a few more healthy sips of coffee, Mom placed her elbows on the table and leaned in.

"If we're not going to talk about your personal life, tell me about work. Classes start Monday, right? Do you think you'll get mistaken for a grad student again this year?"

Last year, my first year as the assistant director in the creative writing program, I was hit on by students all the time, and Mom loved to bring this up. Once they found out who I was, their embarrassment was almost palpable. But it came with the territory of being the youngest assistant director the department had ever had.

"Not sure. I guess we'll see." My colleagues and I had spent the last two weeks in training, preparing for the arrival of students back on campus to breathe the life-blood into the prestigious university and into our dusty old offices.

I had a good feeling about this year. And I loved what I did. I was an assistant director in the academic advising office. So, while the advisers who worked for me helped the undergraduate students with transferring credits and enrolling in courses, I oversaw the handful of graduate students we had each year, taking a personal interest in their success. It was a pretty low-key job that allowed me to work on the book I'd been writing for the past two years now.

"And you're still thinking about New York?" she asked.

I nodded. "That's the plan." After this academic year was over, my plan was to leave my job at the university and move to New York City where I could focus on my writing career and finally finish my manuscript.

I finished off the rest of my coffee and got up to toss

the empty cup, then gave my mom a kiss on the cheek.

"Sorry to head out early, Mom," I said, lucky to have an excuse at the ready. "I've got meetings back on campus." And I'd maxed out on sex life conversations with my mother for the day.

"Bye, Zachary." Mom smiled warmly at me, watching me go.

As I climbed into my car for the drive over to campus, I mentally noted that it was Friday. Maybe I'd take her suggestion after all and go out tonight. You never knew when you might just meet the one.

Chapter Two

Poppy

I shouldn't have let Jodee drag me here. That much was certain. As we walked through the living room, I dodged a ping-pong ball as it went sailing past our heads from a nearby game of beer pong. *Why had I let her talk me into this?*

"Aren't you glad we came?" Jodee grinned excitedly and handed me a beer. I moved in next door to her a few weeks ago. We were both about to begin our master's program—me in poetry, and her in creative non-fiction—but that was where our similarities ended. My life came with a lot of complications and added responsibility as the result of a one-time mistake that hers did not. I knew she wouldn't get it, but there was a hint of underlying anxiety I felt about being away from home.

But since I had a rare, free-night before classes started Monday, and Jodee couldn't fathom the idea of me moping around at home alone on a Friday night, here I was.

"Not particularly. I don't do college parties." Not

even in my undergrad days.

Jodee rolled her eyes. "It's not a college party. It's a house party. And it's practically tradition."

That part may have been true. We attended a tiny, but prestigious East coast university in a little town with only a handful of bars. The bar scene got old, too, so house parties were pretty commonplace. My attendance at them, however, was not. I'd gone here for undergrad too, but as a commuter student still living at home with my parents.

"Guys are so weird," I said, as two particularly preppy-looking guys in front of us started shot-gunning beers.

"I think they're kind of cute," Jodee said, grinning at one of them over her drink. "Besides, you're only saying that because of Jason."

I knew she was right, so I didn't say anything. Ever since Jason dumped me out of the blue, I hadn't been myself. Especially around men. Maybe if he'd given me a reason I could have moved on, but he just told me it wasn't working out, that it was "him, not me." It was bullshit, like the whole time we'd been together had meant nothing, and I'd only gotten more upset since it happened last month. We'd made a lot of plans together over our year-long relationship, but I didn't realize Jason was making plans of his own, too. And one of them was to dump me shortly after my twenty-fourth birthday.

Jodee turned to me. "Look, I know you aren't stoked to be here right now, but I think this will help." She grabbed my arm in excitement. "I know. You should hook up with one of these guys. That's the best way to get over an ex. I'll help you find someone."

I needed a man like I needed a second period each month. "I'm swearing off men," I said to her, but it was useless. She was already peering through the crowd, even standing on tiptoes to look around. She pointed toward the door. "Look at that guy. He's cute, right?" I tried to see who she was talking about but there were too many people crowding the party.

"Oh, wait, he's with a girl. Damn it."

The crowd parted, and my heart stopped. The room went dead silent; my ears were ringing, and I felt like I might throw up. My ex, Jason, had just walked into the party. And he wasn't alone. Trailing behind him was his new girlfriend, the one he started dating about three seconds after we broke up. Of all the fuckery. Why were they here? Was there seriously nothing else to do tonight?

I spun around and grabbed Jodee's arm, whispering, "Jodee. That's Jason."

She stared for a second, confused, and I saw her putting the pieces together as her eyes widened.

"No way," she said, narrowing her eyes in their direction. "Well, you're way prettier than her."

They started walking toward us, but hadn't seen us yet. Luckily, they were distracted by someone Jason knew. I felt like I'd been struck dumb, my mind was totally blanking. Thankfully, Jodee stepped in.

"Okay, what should we do? Do you want to leave?"

I thought about it. There was a back door ... I could escape like Andy tunneling his way out of Shawshank with my dignity still firmly intact. I was about to open my mouth to tell her that when I realized I was being a coward. And I was not a coward. I was a strong ass woman and I wasn't about to flee with my tail between my legs.

I turned to Jodee, my brows knit tightly in

determination. "No. We should stay."

"Are you sure? Really, I understand if you don't want to be here, exes are a nightmare." Jodee's concerned eyes continued scanning my face for any trace of hesitation. I knew she was just looking out for me, but her concern made me even more resolute.

"Positive. There's no way I'm letting some dickhead scare me off that easily."

Her eyebrows shot up in surprise, a forced, hesitant grin on her face. "If you say so..."

Suddenly, I had an idea. "What's that saying ... Don't get mad, get even?"

Jodee's smile faded. "Poppy..."

I didn't wait for her to finish. This wasn't a moment for second-guessing.

"Don't worry, I have a plan." When one of the preppy-looking guys started waving her over to their beer pong game, I gave her a tiny push in their direction as she gave me a concerned look. "Go play. Seriously. I'll be fine. I've got this."

She agreed, but before she headed off to play the

obnoxious drinking game she made me promise to tell her if I needed her. I started scanning the party, looking for the right guy, all the while my lady balls growing larger with every beat of the bass that was coming out of the speakers. Then, I saw him, standing by the stairs. He was tall, at least six-foot-two, with dark hair that seemed effortlessly messy and groomed at the same time. His defined jawline was dusted with dark stubble, and he looked to be in his late twenties. *Perfect. Hot as hell and obviously not one of these idiot college kids.* Maybe he'd understand this insane predicament I was about to put him in.

He turned in my direction for a moment, and I felt my mouth drop open as my gaze met his seductive, emerald green eyes fringed with black lashes. Just looking at him made me feel like I'd committed a sin. Like maybe I needed to head to the nearest confessional and unload all my dirty little secrets to whoever would listen and could atone me for my impure thoughts.

I didn't stop to think. I was being drawn to him in a way that was completely out of my control. As I got closer, I could have high-fived myself. He was so ridiculously attractive—I'm talking Abercrombie model attractive—that I knew he'd be the perfect sucker punch to Jason and his new whore. Never mind that this guy was totally out of my league in real life. This was make-believe. My make-believe…and I was about to *make Jason believe* that we were an item.

He was talking to someone else, but that didn't matter to me. All social decency had gone out the window the moment I'd decided on my plan. I tapped him on the shoulder and tried to look normal. He turned to me, looking down as though amused at me standing all of five-foot-nothing in my ballet flats. When our gazes collided, nothing could have prepared me for the wave of desire that surged through me as we locked eyes for the first time. The room tipped sideways as the full-weight of his sexual prowess hit me.

Hefting up my lady balls for what I was about to do, I took a moment to compose myself, clearing my throat.

"Look," I said, as he observed me with a slight smile, "I know you don't know me, but my ex just walked in with his new girlfriend, and he's a total asshole, so I need you to pretend to be my date."

He paused for a moment, and I had a flash of fear that he might tell me to get lost, but then he grinned, revealing a row of straight, white teeth that couldn't have been more perfect if they'd been featured in an advertisement for orthodontics.

"Just one question." His voice was deep and confident and sent another shockwave of lust rushing through me. My God, this man is hitting me in all the right places and I know I should back away, tuck my lady balls back into their appropriate hiding spot and run. But I was already so far in this that backing down wasn't an option the moment we locked eyes.

My heart dropped into my stomach. "Sure."

"Can I at least know your name before we start dating?"

I let out a relieved laugh and held out my hand. "It's Poppy."

He tested my name on his lips, and I very much liked the sound of it. He wrapped his hand around mine and my stomach did a backflip—a backflip because I was suddenly in way over my head, or because I was really going through with this mission to show Jason how quickly I'd moved on too.

"Zach."

The way he looked at me made my mouth go dry, and it was all too easy to imagine his hands doing exactly what his eyes just did, running up and down my body, eventually reaching my.... *Get a grip*, I thought, stunned by my own intense reaction.

I shook myself out of it. All I was here to do was make Jason jealous, not to swoon over some other guy. I motioned toward the kitchen. "Well, I guess you can start by getting me a drink."

"I like a woman who knows how to take control," he said, and my heartbeat kicked up a few notches. I swallowed. Zach flashed that panty-dropping grin again and led me through the crowd, but it was so densely packed like pheromone-soaked sardines in a can. He reached back and grabbed my hand, sending butterflies rushing to the pit of my stomach.

After we'd gotten our drinks, we opted to forego the suffocating interior and settled into the backyard. It was impossible not to notice how romantic it was to be secluded in a corner of the yard, standing underneath rows of string lights that highlighted the colorful array of fall leaves. Jason was nowhere in sight, but I was finding myself not minding that too much.

"I usually have to work a little harder than this to pick up a girl," Zach said, and I felt myself grinning. I found that hard to believe, considering that I couldn't even look at him without picturing myself on top of him, underneath him, in bed with him, running my tongue along his well-defined pecs. It didn't help that the shirt and tailored jeans he wore were accentuating his perfectly toned body. I caught a wave of his scent. It was crisp, and decidedly masculine.

It took a moment for me to realize he'd asked me how I ended up at the party. I tried to keep my voice from betraying my thoughts as I said, "My friend dragged me here, to be honest."

He grinned again. That grin alone was enough to make me wet. *Jesus.*

"So, this ex of yours … should I go kick his ass, or…?" He interrupted my thoughts, then paused, waiting for my reaction. The story of my ex dumping me for another woman wasn't exactly what I wanted to discuss with the painfully sexy guy I just met and begged to be my 'make-believe boyfriend' for the night.

"No, it's okay. We dated for a year, and then he just

broke it off. It was kind of out of the blue." I shrugged, trying to portray the candid indifference that my demeanor suggested. Yeah, nope, his rejection still stung. Especially because I suspected the real reason for our break-up and I hated to think of my situation being at the root of our separation.

It seemed impossible, but Zach's face was somehow more beautiful when he was being serious. His eyes more piercing, his full lips parted.

"You weren't kidding about him being an asshole. Well, he must be an idiot if he let you get away."

I stared pointedly at him. "That is seriously the worst pick-up line—like, ever."

He laughed and took another sip of his beer. "Listen, you caught me off guard. I didn't expect to have to impress my 'brand-new girlfriend' when I came out tonight."

"That's fair. Thanks for being a good sport and playing along."

Zach took a sip of his beer. "That's what I'm here for. No, really. I'm actually here to inconspicuously keep an eye on my buddy's little brother. He was the dumbass shot-gunning a beer inside."

I nodded. "So, you're babysitting."

"Pretty much."

"Do we need to go back inside then?" I asked, hoping not because I much preferred the quiet out here to the party inside and the surprising comfort that was developing between me and this virtual stranger, even though we'd only been out here a short time.

Zach shook his head. "Josh is a good kid. He'll have a massive hangover tomorrow, but he won't do anything stupid. And I already snatched his car keys when I got here." He patted his jeans pocket and I silently begged myself not to look at his crotch. *Don't do it. Don't you dare fucking do it, Poppy.*

"Plus, I think my presence alone is enough to deter him from any further bad behavior," he added, drawing my gaze back up to his.

Zach wasn't exactly imposing, but he was tall and muscular, so if he needed to, he could certainly put another man in his place.

"So, tell me, are there things I should know about my

new date … hobbies? Interests? Strange fetishes?"

I smiled. "Fetishes are really more of a second date topic. As for hobbies …" I shrugged. "Reading books. Attempting to write them."

Zach returned my easy smile. It was crazy how natural our conversation felt. "Please don't tell me you write those horrible vampire romances."

"So judgy." I shook my head, frowning in mock disgust. "I may have. In high school. And if you tell anyone that—I'll hunt you down and kill you."

This earned me a laugh out of him, and I immediately decided I liked the sound way too much. "Okay. I can't fault you there. I wrote some pretty awful sci-fi back then."

Our shared interest of writing was intriguing, and while I was sure we could have talked about it easily for another hour, Zach changed the subject, and we bounced from topic to topic, finding more things in common as we did.

"I'm making an assumption here, but since you are at this party I'm assuming you're a student at Vanderburg, right?"

I nodded.

"What are you studying?"

Before I could answer, Jason and his girlfriend walked into the backyard.

"That's them," I hissed at Zach. I wasn't sure what to do. Just act casual? Or should I grab Zach's hand? Suddenly, this whole idea seemed a tad dramatic. But Zach had his own idea. Just as my pencil-dick ex was about to look our way, Zach turned my face toward his. His warm palm rested on my cheek and I stared up at him helplessly.

In the span of a moment, I knew his lips were about to descend on mine, and my ovaries did a little happy dance. Suddenly coming to this stupid party seemed like the best idea ever.

And when he leaned down and pressed his lips to mine? Every thought left my brain, including Jason, his new girlfriend, and the mountain of responsibility in my life. I was totally blinded by the rush of desire that surged through my body, settling deep inside my core. His lips were full and soft, and when he nibbled against my lower lip, I put my arms around his neck just to keep my legs from giving out. *Holy fuck!* The man could kiss.

My lips parted in silent invitation and Zach responded, making a tiny grunt of approval before his tongue slid against mine. My body throbbed from the top of my head, through my nipples, which were now two hard pinpricks beneath my shirt, and even farther down, between my legs. His strong hands landed on my hips and pulled me in closer and I had to stop myself from moaning.

I could feel his hard, muscular body through his shirt as I pressed against him, sliding a hand down his chest to his stomach, lightly running my fingers over his six pack. Our bodies were touching in all the right places and I swear I could feel a bulge there…a bulge that I wasn't sure I was the cause of, or if this was his 'normal' state. I wasn't sure but in that moment, I wanted to find out— with or without Jason and his bimbo watching. The lady balls were growing larger with every pant and moan of our kiss.

It was all I could do to keep from reaching down into his pants right then and there. The desire to pet his one-eyed python was a sharp pulse of need. I was so not normally like this…this wanton woman willing to throw caution to the wind and grope and pull at anything with an XY chromosome. I was a serious graduate student who read two hundred books a year and didn't even own a vibrator. I didn't go all weak over a man. Ever.

But this guy? It was like his presence had set up shop in my womb, and my lady parts were ready to roll out the welcome-wagon for him.

I could have stayed like that forever, drunk on him and hanging on for dear life, but moments later, the kiss ended, and I felt like I'd just been slapped in the face.

We looked at each other, breathing heavily. It was like he was the only person in the world who existed in this moment. Then I blinked, and it felt like someone turned the party back on because I was suddenly remembering where we are and why we were here. I didn't even check to see if Jason was still around. It seemed stupid that I ever cared. That was the best kiss of my entire life, and it was with a complete stranger.

"Shit, that was…" he started, his voice deeper, slightly breathless.

"Yeah," I added, dumbly, touching a finger to my trembling, and still-damp lips.

When I did finally have my wits about me enough to look, I noticed that Jason and his new girlfriend were conspicuously absent.

Before either of us could say anything else, we were interrupted by Jodee.

"There you are. I've been looking for you."

I turned in her direction, my hand falling away from my mouth.

"You were right, this party is lame. I'm going to head out soon," she said, glancing at Zach and I could tell she was dying to hear what I was doing out here with this man.

I looked back at Zach. "Um, thanks," I stammered, not sure what else to say. This guy was like an orgasm on two legs, and I was having a hard time keeping my cool.

"We're breaking up already?" He grinned, and just as I was getting the feeling back in my legs, I melted again.

I smiled back. "Looks like it."

"I should at least take you out on a proper date some time." That sexy, deep voice, nearly took my breath away. Every part of my body was screaming yes, especially my lower half, but I forced myself to keep calm and collected.

"I don't know if that's a good idea…" I saved him the lecture about how I just got out of a relationship, and how I wanted to buckle down and focus on my writing, and all the rest of it … and just left it at that. He had to know that the make-believe role I'd asked him to portray tonight was explanation enough that a relationship—hell, even a date—was something I was avoiding like the plague.

"Can I at least get your number?" He smiled, and I pictured leading him into my bedroom and ripping his clothes off. *Bad, Poppy.* I shook my head, trying to get ahold of myself. *What is wrong with me?* I just met this guy and I already can't stop thinking about fucking him. And, sure, he's sweet, funny and basically a human aphrodisiac, but I needed to relax. Jason really did mess with my head, if this was how I was acting. *You've sworn off men, remember?* So even though the last thing I want to do is walk away from the sexiest guy I've ever met, I forced myself to say, "Sorry, I'm not really looking for anything romantic right now."

He nodded. "I understand."

I thought I detected a hint of disappointment in his voice.

I started to walk away, then turned back. I was caught off guard all over again at the sight of his arresting green eyes and sensuous lips, but I put on a smile. "Who knows, if it's meant to be, maybe we'll meet again."

Zach smiled, and nodded once like he believed me.

As I walked out of the party I could feel his gaze smoldering through me and even though it was a warm night, I shivered. I might have sworn off men, but I was pretty sure Zach would be creeping into my fantasies later that night. My stupid ovaries were clapping their hands and dancing like Ellen had just given us a brand-new car.

I didn't know if we'd ever see each other again, but I did know one thing—I'd never felt anything like that kiss before in my entire life and was almost certain I never would again. But the tightening feeling in my chest, and the realization that lightning didn't often strike twice— well, I'd just have to find a way to push those from my brain, because I really didn't have room for another man in my life. Connor was enough. Wasn't he?

Chapter Three

Zach

The morning sun did nothing to erase my impure thoughts of Poppy. The entire drive to campus that morning I couldn't stop my mind from replaying thoughts of meeting her at the party over the weekend. The way she'd taken charge, practically telling me I was going to be her pretend boyfriend, rather than asking if I could. It had been rather cute, and now, even without hardly knowing anything about her, I was somehow already smitten by the mysterious girl with her dark hair and serious eyes.

I'd hardly recovered from my last relationship and now here I was pining over someone who I'd probably never see again. This was a university of ten-thousand students. We never got around to discussing her program of study before I catapulted myself headfirst into lust with that kiss. The odds were not in our favor. And, yeah, she was a student, so I probably shouldn't have used her as spank-bank material all weekend, but I had.

Fucking sue me.

She was gorgeous. Petite and nervous and lovely.

Men had written sonnets about women less striking.

I spent the whole weekend trying to write with a head full of her, and a serious hard on.

But today was the first day of classes, which meant my morning would be occupied by meetings with each of the new graduate students, so there would be little time for impure thoughts. Back to business, as it were.

When I got to my office, I immediately closed the door, as if someone would see it in my eyes that my mind was on anything but my morning meetings.

Fucking pull it together, Zach.

Apparently, my mom had been right. But it wasn't my aura that was out of whack, it was an appendage much farther south. Too bad there was no time to beat it into shape. No pun intended. I'd never had a single kiss fuck with my head so badly before.

And I wasn't sure what I expected from Poppy when she approached, but from the first moment she opened her mouth and spoke, I knew she was different.

Her voice wasn't high-pitched or girly, even though her frame was petite and delicate. Instead, her tone was deeper than I expected, almost raspy and seductive. I liked it immediately. I could have listened to her talk for hours — listened to her recite Tolstoy, or the fucking alphabet, for that matter. I just wanted to be near her.

I hadn't wanted to go out that night at all—especially not to some ridiculous keg-party where I was babysitting my friend's kid brother—but everything changed the moment Poppy walked up to me with her interesting proposal. And of course, I was all too happy to play along.

She was easy to talk to—we chatted about wide ranging topics from Darwinism to our favorite authors, both agreeing that the concept of having an actual favorite book was the most absurd idea we'd ever heard. Her eyes lit up when she spoke, her lips twitching when she got excited—she was mesmerizing.

A smile played on my own lips, remembering how she admitted that she liked to write young adult vampire romance, and then threatened me within an inch of my life if I ever told anyone that. I'd felt inspired enough to admit my early, atrocious attempts at writing bad sci-fi when I was still in high school. Poppy had laughed, her eyes sparkling on mine.

A knock on the door interrupted my memory. I

glanced at my watch—8:50. *Shit.* I wasn't sure if I was impressed or annoyed at the early arrival. I could've used that extra ten minutes to prepare for the meeting, or at the very least, take a mental cold shower by going over my plans for the day. I reached for the stack of papers that was already accumulating on my desk—who was this student again? A poet in the master's program that I'd be advising. I hadn't even taken the time to review the file. Whatever. It'd be fine. I stepped out from behind my desk and swung the door open.

"Good morning …" my words died on my lips.

It was Poppy.

Heat prickled down my spine—a mix between lust and fear. I wanted her, yes. But could I really remain objective and professional working alongside her? Did I even want to try?

Her honey brown eyes locked with mine the same way they had at the party, but this time, instead of watching them flicker in interest, I saw them widen with surprise. The color drained from her cheeks as I let myself give her a quick once-over—she was dressed more casually than she'd been on Friday night in a pair of jeans and a t-shirt, and she wore a hint of pink lip-gloss that I couldn't help but imagine smeared all over my cock.

Jesus, Zach. There goes my mental cold shower right out the window.

"Poppy." Her name on my lips was a soft murmur. I cleared my throat to start again. "You said we'd met again." If it was meant to be … I didn't add that last part, as I was pretty sure those words were coming back to bite her in the ass.

She blinked at me, the apples of her cheeks now a pretty shade that nearly matched her lips. And those lips… Christ. They were now parted as she drew a slow, shaky inhale.

"Come inside?"

She stood rooted in place. "This has to be some mistake."

"Poppy Ellis, poetry grad student," I read aloud from the folder I realized was still in my hands. "Welcome to the program. I'll be your adviser."

Swallowing a lump in her throat, Poppy gave a slow, solemn nod and followed me through the office door.

"Have a seat."

She obeyed, hesitantly lowering herself into the chair in front of my desk while I took the one behind it. "'I'm sorry, but there's got to be someone else I can work with." Her eyes darted around my office, refusing to settle back on me. I waited patiently until they locked with mine again. Electric. She immediately looked back down at her hands.

She was perfection. Those soft waves of hair and honey-colored eyes. I wanted to drink her in. Instead, I focused on doing something useful—rolling up the sleeves of my dress shirt—since the room had suddenly become about ten degrees too warm.

I couldn't help but notice the way her eyes clung to my forearms, or the ink that decorated them. Various quotes, short poems I'd written, my favorite philosophers' prose scrawled in Latin. My tattoos were very personal to me that way, and suddenly I was regretting exposing so much of myself. I was the kind of man who needed to touch something in order to understand it, but rather than running my fingertips over the words, letting them ground me, I wanted to touch the young woman seated before me in a desperate attempt to understand her.

Of course, physical contact with students was not on

the agenda, so I did the next best thing in an attempt to make myself useful. I thumbed through her file. She had already won several awards for her poetry, and a few of her pieces had been picked up by some prominent literary magazines. In that instant I knew it had to be me—the other advisor for her program hated poetry and he was a grade-A asshole. I tried to tell myself it had nothing to do with feeling possessive over her—though the idea of someone else mentoring her made me want to put my fist through a wall.

Decision made, I composed myself. "You're a pretty impressive poet, Poppy, and I'm the most published poetry advisor on staff." I let her file fall closed as I met her gaze again. "Seems like you and I are a perfect fit."

She tucked her hair behind her ear and shook her head. "I just don't know. I mean, how are we supposed to work together after I practically begged you to be my fake boyfriend for a night, and then, well, you know."

No way was she going to get away with not saying it out loud.

"Know what?"

She rolled her eyes. "The kiss, Zach."

"It was a kiss," I said, totally downplaying how I felt about said kiss. I could write an entire novel about that kiss. "And it's not like it took much convincing to play along to make your ex jealous. You're gorgeous, Poppy. But still, it was just a kiss. I'm not going to let it get in the way of us working together."

She closed her eyes for a second and took a deep breath. "Alright," she said. "I guess we can give it a shot."

This time, when I stuck out my hand, she shook it. I pretended not to feel goose bumps racing up my arm.

"Well, now that that's settled, could I convince you to take this discussion somewhere I can grab a cup of coffee? The cup I had earlier isn't cutting it today."

Poppy had already grabbed her purse before I could even finish my sentence. "I'm dying for coffee," she admitted. "I can't stand Mondays and I might go postal if I don't get some caffeine in my system."

"Coffee it is," I said, escorting her from my office. We settled on a coffee shop just a short walk away on campus.

"Drink's on me," I said, motioning for her to grab a seat.

"You don't have to do that."

I shrugged. "Consider it a welcome to the program. What would you like?"

She furrowed her brow but didn't fight me on it. "Just coffee please. Black."

I ordered us each a large mug of coffee and stuffed a ten-dollar tip in the jar for good karma. Poppy had already settled in at a small table in the far back of the shop. I joined her, sliding her mug across the table. "Is this big enough to get you through a Monday?"

She smiled. "Maybe after the second or third refill. Thanks."

I nodded toward the notebook she still had pressed against her chest. "Anything good in there?"

She blushed, setting the notebook on the table and opening it to a list of goals for the year. Not quite the poems I was hoping for, but instead everything she was looking to accomplish this year at Vanderburg. Ah, so she was one of those people. A list maker. I preferred to let things ride and see where I ended up, believing that the journey was just as good as the destination. But I enjoyed listening to her talk, enjoyed the self-conscious way she tucked her hair behind her ear, the way she led the conversation, and especially the way her neck and chest grew splotchy with pink flushes of color the few times she was bold enough to meet my watchful gaze.

Still, I hungered to see her poetry. To see her words on the page, bold and exposing as I knew they would be. I was dying to know what she wrote about. Something mundane like the changing fall leaves, or something serious like her relationship with her father, or something romantic like falling in love. I wondered if after her breakup, did her writing turn dark and morose, speaking from a place of a broken heart.

What little I knew about her, Poppy was a serious girl, but I wanted to know if she had a softer, more romantic side too. A reckless side. Shit, I didn't know what it was about this girl, but I wanted to know about each and every one of her sides, examine them in the moonlight. Study them in the morning dawn while she stirred awake next to me.

Once she was finished reading over everything she was looking to get out of the program, she talked about her past work, and her publishing goals. I caught about every third or fourth word, and more than anything else I was intent on that pink lip-gloss and the thoughts of her waking in my bed with that mouth forming the sounds of pleasure as she came. So much for keeping work life and personal life separate but I was unable to stop myself.

"Right?" she said, blowing softly into her mug of coffee before taking a sip.

Shit. I had stopped listening. "Sorry, what was that?"

"I said that I promise I'll stay professional about this," she said, sounding like she was trying to convince herself. "You said you would, too, right?"

I couldn't help but smile. "I said that I wouldn't let what happened Friday night get in the way of us working together. I'll help you achieve your goals in any way I can, but I didn't say anything about staying professional. We're two grown adults, Poppy."

She looked at me with curiosity. "How old are you by the way?"

"Twenty-nine. I'll be thirty in March." As my mother kept reminding me.

"You don't look it."

I nodded. "I've been told that a lot."

"So, no wife and kids for you?"

I got the sense that she expected me to say no, either that I wasn't ready, or I wasn't interested. But neither of those things were true.

"Not yet. But hopefully someday soon. What about you? How old are you?"

"Twenty-four," she said softly, still watching me.

I nodded. Plenty old enough to know what she was doing. "As I said, we're two grown adults. With an assload of sexual tension."

"An assload?" She rolled her eyes.

"I believe that's the technical term, yes."

Her eyebrows darted up in surprise.

I had a feeling I would enjoy working with Poppy much more than was appropriate.

Chapter Four

Poppy

"Have fun tonight, buddy." I ran my fingers through Connor's hair, and watched as his mouth quirked up in a grin. This little freckled face was my whole world—and the reason why I worked so hard.

"Love ya, Mom!" Connor all but sprinted out the front door and out to the driveway where my mom's car was parked.

Connor had his soccer team's pizza party tonight and my parents had volunteered to take him. I stopped on the front porch and waved to my parents through the windshield while Connor climbed into the backseat.

I loved my son with all my heart, but deep down, a very small part of me wished he'd waited until later in my life to make his appearance. One fateful night my whole world changed. My teenage boyfriend and I were in love, and I trusted him. And I had no reason to doubt him that night when he said he'd put on the condom. I'd even heard the crinkle of the wrapper. The next month when I told him I was pregnant, and questioned how that could have happened, his face went white. Then he'd admitted the truth—that he'd never put it on at all. But none of that mattered now. Because while he got to go off and live his life with no responsibility whatsoever, mine had been irrevocably changed.

I wasn't ready for a baby at seventeen, any more than I was ready at twenty-four to be the mom of a seven-year-old. But I did the best I could, which included juggling school for us both, his sports, work, and motherhood. And now I was so attached to him, to his sweet presence in my life, that the thought of spending an evening alone was the most depressing thing I could imagine. Which was why I'd invited my neighbors over for dinner later.

No sooner than I was back inside, the sound of the doorbell had me heading for the front door again.

Jodee grinned and pulled me into a one-armed hug. Behind her Kody walked in carrying several bags. He exuded so much energy it felt like a gust of wind came in behind him.

"Hey, girl, hey," he said, voice cheery.

We headed toward the kitchen together.

They'd met Connor a couple of times and were sweet

with him and understanding about the fact that I was mostly a homebody.

"Booze," Kody said when he saw me staring at all the bags.

Thank God. After the day I'd had, I could use a cocktail. Or three.

I had a rule for myself that I didn't drink alcohol during the week, but I had a feeling this year I'd be breaking a lot of my self-imposed rules.

Jodee came into the room as Kody was pouring our first round. He was starting us off with cosmopolitans, he explained.

"Monday funday," Kody sang as he vigorously shook up the cocktails.

"I don't think that's a thing," Jodee said, ever the practical one.

"It is now." He poured the mixture into three individual glasses and garnished them with a lime wedge.

"I'm impressed," I said after taking a large sip.

"I bartended for three years at a gay club downtown," he said with a wink. "I made a lot of cosmos."

We met only weeks ago when Connor and I moved into our place and Jodee and Kody immediately came over to help us move furniture and unpack boxes. Now, it felt like we'd been friends for years.

"Kody, I have to ask…" Jodee paused, a little embarrassed. "Are you gay?"

While Kody's impeccable sense of style, bleached blond hair and pierced ears had me wondering the same thing, I wasn't about to ask. I glanced at Kody, hoping he wasn't offended. He paused, looking at Jodee with raised eyebrows. Then he grinned. "Honey, I'm fabulous."

We burst into laughter.

"I can't believe you two went to a party and didn't tell me," Kody pouted, and my heart skipped a beat. He was talking, of course, about the party Jodee dragged me to last Friday night. The party where I met Zach. My mouth went dry at the memory of him flashing that flirtatious, heart stopping smirk in my direction. The one that nearly had me ripping his clothes off after knowing him for five minutes.

I could still feel his body pressed against mine, his

full lips left me aching. My body tingled at the very thought of him. After spending more time with him in his office, and at the coffee shop, I have nearly every detail committed to memory. His dark hair that was just long enough to run your fingers through, his full lips, strong jawline and that rugged bit of facial hair. My fingertips tingled with the memory of touching his sinfully hard abs and chest through his shirt. And those arresting green eyes… Speaking of arresting, I could think of a few things I'd like to do with him that involved a pair of handcuffs. *Jesus, Poppy.*

I forced myself to tune back into the conversation. Just the thought of Zach threatened to totally overwhelm everything else, and the last thing I needed was for Kody or Jodee to catch the look on my face as I fantasized about him.

"Ladies, I have a surprise." Kody reached into his bag and pulled out a bottle of tequila, which he set on the table with a grin. "Who wants a tequila shooter?"

I almost refused. *Tequila on a Monday night?* Then decided why the hell not? One wouldn't kill me, and it might be just the thing to get me to loosen up.

Jodee and I grinned and raised our hands like we were in class. As Kody poured the shooters, I cut up more limes and grabbed the salt from the kitchen. As I walked back into the living room, I heard Kody insisting we skip over the "get to know you" phase of friendship.

"It's a huge bore. Nobody likes small talk. I have a better idea." He passed each of us a glass. "Why don't we go around and say our best and worst quality. I'll start. My best quality is that, like I said, I'm fabulous." He did a pretend hair flip. "And my worst quality is that I love reality TV and binge watch it way too much."

We licked the salt off our hands, downed the shooters and sucked on the limes, grimacing from the strong liquor. I only drank half of mine, needing to maintain some level of composure.

"Okay," Jodee jumped in. "My best quality is my sense of reason." Kody and I snickered, already aware of how pragmatic Jodee could be. She laughed with us. "It's true. And my worst quality is that my hair falls out everywhere and clogs the shower drain."

We laughed, and then I realized it was my turn.

"My best quality is that I make the best batch of

chocolate chip cookies in the world. And my worst quality is that I'll eat the whole thing if somebody doesn't stop me."

"Cheers to new friends." Kody held up his tequila shooter and Jodee and I followed suit. After we've finished the second round, Kody held up one hand, commanding the floor.

"And one more thing. Can we all agree right now not to be weird about farting in front of each other?"

Jodee and I laughed, caught off guard. We both shrugged when we realized he was serious.

"I guess that's fine," I said.

Kody's mouth curled into a grin and he passed gas loudly. "Thank God, I've been holding that in for the past half hour."

We all cracked up again, and once we'd calmed down we decided to start making dinner. Jodee was a dairy-free vegetarian, and Kody was a vegan currently on one of those fad diets where you eat high protein, low carb. I thought it would take a miracle to find a meal we could all eat, but luckily, it's Kody's "cheat day" so I bought ingredients for a few of my favorite dishes—my best friend in undergrad had been a vegan, too, so I knew the drill. Since I rarely went out we often cooked together at my parents' house and enjoyed an evening in. Tonight, we were having "zoodles" with pesto and soy crumbles and buffalo cauliflower bites with vegan bleu cheese.

I gave Kody the task of creating the "zoodles" from zucchini, handed Jodee a knife to cut up the cauliflower and started preparing the vegan bleu cheese. As I stirred the tahini, lemon juice, garlic, and vinegar in a bowl, my hips pressed against the counter and I had a sudden flashback to Zach pulling my hips against his as we kissed. I held in a gasp as I was blinded by a sudden flash of desire. My heartbeat quickened as I imagined his large, muscular body against mine, his strong hands wrapping around me, then lifting my shirt over my head and removing my bra as his tongue moved from my mouth, down to my shoulders and finally my breasts. *Fuck.*

I glanced at Jodee and Kody, who hadn't noticed my flushed face and heavy breathing over the upbeat pop music Kody put on. *Seriously, what is wrong with me?* I struggled to keep calm while I finished making the bleu cheese. Luckily, Kody interrupted my thoughts.

"Poppy, can you check if I'm doing this right? Is it

supposed to be this much of a mess?"

I welcomed the distraction. I couldn't keep thinking about Zach or I was going to completely lose my mind. In fact, the only way I was allowed to think of him from this point forward was as my adviser.

Luckily, I made it through the meal prep, vowing not to think about Zach for the rest of the night. Once we'd finished cooking, we settled back into the living room to eat balancing our plates on our knees and opting to keep it casual rather than sit at the dining table.

"This is amazing," Kody said through a mouthful of zoodles and pesto. "I usually just microwave myself something for dinner, so I could get used to this."

"This is so good, Poppy," Jodee added, dipping a piece of cauliflower into the vegan bleu cheese. "By the way, how did your adviser meeting go?"

Shit.

Of course, just when I stop thinking about Zach, he finds a way to get back into my head.

"Um." I felt myself blushing. I considered not admitting the truth, but I'd never been good at keeping secrets, especially from a friend. "Remember the guy from the party Friday night?"

Jodee nodded, looking confused. "Yeah, Zach. What about him?"

"Well," I gulped. "He's my adviser."

"Stop," Jodee said loudly, turning to me with eyes wide and mouth forming a perfect O. "The one you kissed?"

I nodded, knowing the look of guilt on my face was unmistakable.

"Poppy. You told him if it was meant to be you'd see each other again. It's totally meant to be."

She was right, that's exactly what I'd said to him when he asked for my number. I'd almost forgotten about it, but now it was like I was there all over again. I remembered the feeling of his eyes watching me as I walked away from him at the party, and a shiver ran from the top of my head all the way down to my toes at the thought. I shook it off. It didn't mean anything. The whole situation was pure chance.

"Hold on. What's happening? I need details." Kody leaned forward on the edge of his seat. I explained everything. The party, Jason, Jason's new girlfriend, and my brilliant plan to make him jealous that had now gone totally awry.

"So, this guy is your adviser now? That's crazy." Kody was talking a mile a minute, clearly excited by the drama. "What does this guy look like? Is he hot?" *So hot I could hardly keep my clothes on.* Kody looked toward Jodee, who was nodding, then back at me.

"He's tall, with dark hair." My body went numb as I described him. My plan not to think about Zach was totally out the window now and I couldn't stop my pulse from quickening. It was like I was seeing him for the first time all over again. I paused, struggling to maintain my composure.

"And his body?" Kody wasn't letting me off the hook.

"Muscular. Toned arms, strong chest, and amazing abs." I clenched my fists, thinking about running my hands from his shoulders, to his chest and down to his flat stomach. "His eyes are this piercing, emerald green. And he has this sexy smirk he gives when he says something dirty." I swallowed. Maybe it's the tequila, but I just said way more than I intended to.

Kody and Jodee exchange meaningful glances. *I must be losing my mind, saying all of this.* I try to move the topic along, because if I keep talking about Zach's body I'm going to have an orgasm right there on my second-hand couch. I know we all agreed that farting in front of one another was an acceptable friendship practice but I'm pretty sure coming in front of one another would be an unspoken no-no.

"None of this means anything. Plus, he's my adviser." I tried to be the voice of reason.

"Well if you don't want him, I'll take him," Kody interjected with a sly smile.

Jodee refused to let the subject drop. "Things happen for a reason, Poppy. Don't you believe in soul mates?"

I was saved from having to answer by my phone, which chimed whenever I got a new email. When I saw who the sender was, the wind got knocked out of me.

"Excuse me, Poppy, but you look like you just saw a ghost."

I tore my eyes away from the screen and saw Kody watching me.

"What's up?" Jodee asked. "Everything okay?"

They were both staring at me, and I knew there was no way around it, especially after the reaction I just had. I let out a sigh.

"It's just an email." I paused, biting my lip. "From Zach."

Jodee and Kody both sat up straight in their seats. "Well, what does it say?" Jodee asked, almost whispering.

"Just read it out loud," Kody demanded, leaning forward and taking a sip of his tequila shooter.

"It's probably something school-related," I said, trying to minimize their excitement, but it was useless. They were both watching me like I was about to perform a one-woman stand-up comedy show. I downed the rest of the tequila I told myself I wasn't going to finish. Needing the liquid courage and all.

"Okay, here goes."

Poppy,

Thank you for taking the time to meet with me today. I know we're going to have an amazing year. I forgot to mention this earlier, but I thought you might like the poet Ariel Elderson. You can read some of her work online.

Always a pleasure,
Zach

I looked up at them. "See? Totally professional." Even as the words left my mouth, even I didn't really believe them. My heart felt like as if it had been shot straight into my throat and my hands were shaking. I put the phone down before anyone noticed.

"Professional?" Kody asked. "He totally wants you. Why do you think he said, 'Always a pleasure'?" He raises an eyebrow at me. "*Pleasure*, Poppy. That's what's on his mind…his pleasure, your pleasure, sexual pleasure."

"Kody, slow that train down…he's my adviser, nothing more." I heard the words I was saying but they weren't registering in my brain.

"It's so romantic. It shows he's thinking about you," Jodee said, grinning widely. "He's thinking about you at—" she pauses. "What time is it?"

"Nine o'clock," Kody jumped in. "Nobody is thinking about someone after 5 p.m. unless they want to bone them."

"Come on, you guys. Seriously, he's my adviser. This is his job." I wasn't sure who I was trying to convince—them or me.

"Seems like he's taking his job pretty seriously." Kody smirked. "I'm not getting late night emails from my adviser about their favorite poets."

I reread the email, still trying to convince myself that it all meant nothing, that Zach was just doing his job like he would for any other student. The worst thing was that despite my protests, everything they've said is making me melt inside. I thought again about what I said to Zach, that if things were meant to be we'd see each other again. I still didn't know if I believed in fate, but I was finding it harder and harder to deny.

Chapter Five

Zach

After stopping by my office to grab my notes, I headed straight for my weekly meeting with my boss.

Lewis Clybourne, the head of the creative writing department at Vanderburg, may be old enough to remember the publication of the first novel ever made. If I'm exaggerating, it's not by much. Still, even if he has one foot in the grave, he's won several national book awards, so walking into Clybourne's office for a meeting feels a lot like walking on holy ground. With how unholy my thoughts have been lately, I knew my first meeting of the year with Clybourne was bound to be harder than I had been the past week and a half.

When I walked into his office, Clybourne's brows were wrinkled down over his eyes as he pounded at his keyboard, mumbling to himself. Not exactly a master of technology. "Zachary, I thought I had you for nine o'clock. I can't get my damn email to work. Have a seat."

We went over the usual niceties of the beginning of the year small talk, which I always hated. What was the point in discussing our summers when we could get down to work and get out of here? Finally, the conversation steered toward the real reason I was here—discussing this year's new crop of writers.

"Where do we stand? How are your advisees?" he asked at last.

"I really see a lot of promise in all of them," I said, buying myself a little time to open my leather folio and pull out my list of student names I'd printed out. I came prepared, knowing Clybourne was exacting in his standards. All my advisees were talented—you had to be to get into this university—but I worried my head would suddenly go blank, the way it tended to do whenever the topic of Poppy came up.

"I've set up Devon with a professor to get his novel finished by spring. He's someone the university press might want to pick up. And I pulled a few strings to get Maria into the Brit lit seminar. She has doctoral program written all over her."

Clybourne nodded, craning his neck over the desk to get a look at the list of names.

"Have you met with Poppy Ellis yet?"

I tried to keep a poker face, but my dick perked up at the mention of her. *Choose your words wisely, Zach.*

"I'm incredibly impressed with her…"

Smart, interesting, and filled with so much promise. The idea of pushing her, of watching her grow was intoxicating. Then my mind took a detour, cataloging the rest of the things I liked about her… Gorgeous tits. Delicious lips. Fuck me eyes. She had that whole tortured writer way about her that made me want to peel back all her layers. And I did mean all.

"With her publication history, she's definitely some of the strongest talent we have this year," I added.

Nice recovery.

"She's one of the more published students we've had in the program in a long time. I trust that you'll take special interest in nourishing her talent. She could mean great things for the university," Clybourne said.

"Of course."

The meeting wrapped up neatly after we discussed a few creative writing opportunities and an upcoming poetry contest, and I made a clean getaway before I showed a little bit too much "special interest" in Poppy. By the time I made it back to my office, I had been gone for all of thirty minutes and my email inbox was already more packed than a college frat party. I clicked through a few, adding new meetings and advising appointments to my calendar until I spotted one from Poppy with the subject line "Today."

Zach,

Wondering if I should meet you today in your office or if you're thinking coffee again. Let me know.

Best,

Poppy

I kept it professional. The last thing I needed was to leave a paper trail of suggestive emails.

Poppy,

Let's have your meeting at the same coffee shop. Please bring the pieces you've been working on this week.

Zach

I had a solid hour before my meeting with Poppy, plenty of time to get through all these emails, but I closed out of my inbox instead. There was no chance in hell of me getting any other work done knowing I'd be a table's distance away from the woman I'd been getting off to for over a week.

I remembered what she'd said about Mondays, how much she hated them. Maybe I could make this one a little bit better. I opened my folio and neatly tore out a piece of paper. Was writing her something too cliché? Fuck it. I had an hour to churn out a poem that could put even the slightest smile on that pink lip-glossed mouth.

By the time I was finished, I had eight minutes to make it to the coffee shop. Perfect. I left the poem unsigned, and folded it up into my right pocket. I'd slip it in her bag when she wasn't looking, a guarantee that I'd be on her mind later when she found it while digging for a pen in class or pulling out her wallet at the grocery store. Then again, maybe she'd never suspect it was from me.

Our table from last week was empty when I got to the café, so I ordered us the same large, black coffees as last week.

A few minutes later, the bells above the door chimed

and I looked up to see Poppy pushing her way inside. She was dressed in a pair of jeans that highlighted her every curve. They were adorably rolled at the ankles, showing off a pair of vintage sneakers. Her loose gray sweatshirt exposed one slender shoulder and the strap of a lacy bra. She was every co-ed fantasy I've ever had come to life and I had to take a slow, deep breath just to keep from groaning.

Her eyes lit up when she spotted me. I took a sip of my coffee and watched her approach. That sweatshirt was draped perfectly over her tits, which looked like just the right size to fill my hands. As if focusing wasn't already going to be a problem, that visual cemented—and I mean cemented—my current situation.

"Hey," she said, offering me a nervous smile as she approached. I wondered if it would always be like this— the uncertainty when we were around each other. This carefully constructed dance to make sure we didn't cross one of the invisible lines that said we shouldn't be together.

"Hey," I returned. "I got you a coffee." I nodded toward the steaming mug waiting for her on the table.

"Thanks. You didn't have to do that."

She was right—and for any other student, I wouldn't have.

"You mind if I grab something to eat?" she asked, dropping her laptop bag into the chair.

"Of course not."

When she headed toward the counter to place her order, I leaned over the side of the table and slipped the note into her bag.

That hint of anxiety when you knew someone was going to read your words uncoiled low in my gut. Even if Poppy wouldn't know they were *my* words, I felt nervous and slightly anxious. What would she think? As I stared at her bag, and waited for her to return, a moment of regret panged through me. Maybe I shouldn't have left it. Maybe she wouldn't like it. Then I realized this is really the only way I could communicate with her and not be discovered—I certainly couldn't send something like that to her university email.

Seconds later, she returned with a bagel, and settled into the seat across from me. "Thanks. My morning was crazy. I didn't have time for breakfast." After taking a big bite of her bagel, Poppy wiped her mouth with a napkin and offered me another of those shy smiles.

I enjoyed my coffee, and the view—while Poppy took a few more bites of her food, and then composed herself, pulling out a notebook and flipping it open.

Before we had a chance to get down to business, a guy and a girl approached our table, stopping right beside it. The guy, in his mid-twenties with bleached hair, grinned at us with a wide smile, and the girl, who looked to be about the same age, with mocha-colored skin and curly hair was watching me with appraising eyes.

Wait. She was Poppy's friend, I remembered her from the party.

"What are you guys doing here?" Poppy hissed, looking from them, and then back to me.

I raised my eyebrows wondering what was going on. "Hey." I stuck out my hand. "I'm Zach."

"Kody," the guy said, giving my hand a shake. "So, you're the hot adviser?" He winked at me, and I couldn't help my answering chuckle.

"That's me. Just your friendly neighborhood hot

adviser." I was dying to know what else Poppy told them.

"These are my neighbors," Poppy offered, voice shaky.

"I'm Jodee," the girl said, taking my hand once Kody had released it.

"And I'm sure they were just leaving, right, guys?" I'd never heard Poppy's tone more commanding. I was amused, and I didn't even know what was happening.

Kody offered a sly smile. "Oh, I don't know. We were kind of eager to meet this mystery man who's got you all hot and bothered."

A slow smile uncurled on my mouth. "I get you hot?"

Poppy hastily shook her head. "Bothered. As in angry. Annoyed." Her lips pressed into a firm line.

One look back at Kody, who was shaking his head, confirmed the truth.

"Why don't you two pull up a seat. Let's get better acquainted." I rose from my chair and gathered two more from an empty table nearby.

"They can't stay," Poppy said.

"It's fine. We can finish our meeting later." No sooner than I had scooted the chairs over, they were joining us at the table—Kody all smiles and Jodee optimistically curious.

And me? I couldn't wipe the smirk off my face. Only Poppy was frowning. And as much as I hated the idea of upsetting her, I couldn't resist the urge to learn more about the woman from the people who knew her best. An opportunity like this might never come up again. Based on the way they sort of ambushed our table, my guess was they were trying their damnedest to give her a careful shove in the right direction, however reluctant she might be.

"So, she likes me, huh?" I directed my question to Kody, who, as far as I could tell from only knowing the dude thirty seconds, lacked a filter.

"Absolutely not." Poppy leaned forward on the table, pointing one finger toward Kody and shaking her head.

Kody shrugged. "Fine. If little miss isn't interested, I'll throw my name in the ring."

It took a moment for realization to strike, but when it did, I let out a chuckle. "No offense buddy, my equipment is all I can handle, I'd have no idea what to do with yours."

"I could show you," Kody offered.

Silently winching at what was clearly the wrong choice of words on my part, I shook my head. "My dick likes pussy, sorry."

Kody pursed his lips. "Can't blame a guy for trying."

I took a sip of my coffee, and looked to Poppy. Her discomfort was evident, and suddenly I felt like an asshole. This was no longer some fun game, and I didn't want to hurt her. I looked to Kody and Jodee, meeting their eyes across the table. "Your friend is sweet, and smart, and I'm sure she's ready to get back to our meeting, so as entertaining as this was, you'll have to excuse us."

As they rose from their seats, Poppy flipped open her notebook once again, face hot, and began muttering something under her breath.

"We got absolutely nothing accomplished," she said.

"You're right. Give him your number and you guys can set up a make-up meeting," Jodee suggested.

Poppy's gaze snapped up to Jodee. "No. You're not

giving him my number."

Kody leaned down and scribbled Poppy's number on a piece of paper, handing it to me.

"For fuck's sake, Kody," Poppy hissed under her breath.

I wasn't sure I'd ever heard her curse before, and it was hot. Everything she did was intriguing, and I wanted more.

They took their cue to exit, and did so with a wave. Kody blew me an air-kiss as they left.

"Listen, I'm sorry," I said after they were gone.

Poppy wasted no time shoving her things back into her bag. "We were supposed to discuss my upcoming assignment. Unless you've forgotten that I'm studying under the renowned Dr. Peggy Chan?"

I swallowed, feeling like even more of a dick. "I haven't."

"And you do understand I didn't enroll here for your personal amusement? I actually want to be a writer—not just a writer, a *great* writer. I thought you of all people might understand that."

"I do. And I promise I'll make it up to you."

"I've got to get to class. Bye, Zach."

As I watched her go, I was struck by a thought. I'd never had such a visceral reaction to a female before. I mean, my ex didn't even know the difference between Seuss and Salinger. But Poppy. Sweet Poppy. She looked like a character out of a Dickens novel—innocent, intelligent, with a rich backstory and a desire to do good in the world. And I was weak for her. Totally and completely at her mercy. Sure, I wanted to fuck her, but I wanted so much more than that, too. Of course, it was just my luck that the one woman I'd been interested in in over a year wasn't looking for a relationship—and was also one of my students. Shit didn't get more complicated than that.

Chapter Six

Poppy

Remember how much I liked Jodee and Kody? I take it all back. I can't believe they hijacked my meeting with Zach. Not only did we not get anything even remotely useful done, but they pretty much said all the things I didn't want them to say. At least they kept quiet about Connor. I wasn't ready for Zach to know that yet, and I wasn't sure why, but I felt oddly defensive of him, of our situation. It was the mama-bear in me, I guess.

Lying on my bed feeling a mixture of regret and anxiety, I wished things could go back to the way they were before I'd met Zach, and everything had become so complicated. But even as I had the thought, I knew it wasn't really how I felt.

"Hey, Poppy, can I use some of your flour?" Jodee shouted from down the hall, interrupting my thoughts.

"Sure, whatever," I shouted back, unable to keep the edge out of my voice.

"What's with the attitude?" Kody had come to stand

in my doorway, his hand on his hip. He had his bleached hair gelled back and was wearing the tightest jeans I'd ever seen on a man.

"I'm just busy with this," I mumbled, gesturing toward my laptop. I still hadn't forgiven them, and I was having a hard time hiding it. In this moment, however, I was really regretting telling them to come over whenever they pleased.

A quick glance to the living room confirmed that Connor was still doing his homework at the coffee table.

"You know what would help?" Kody smiled, totally ignoring the fact that I was clearly trying to work. He leaned down to whisper near my ear. "If you got laid."

"I agree," Jodee said, closer now.

I ignored them and kept typing.

"You've been so on edge lately. Are you horny?" Kody sat down at the dining table beside me. His question was almost laughable, considering the fact that I could hardly keep my hands to myself every time I laid eyes on Zach.

"Can I please just do my work?" I asked, clearly frustrated. The last thing I needed was for Connor to overhear any of this. "Plus, there are little ears nearby." I looked pointedly toward the living room.

Kody stood, putting his hands up in mock surrender, and left, with Jodee in tow.

It wasn't a total lie; I did need to get work done. I'd taken a part-time job to pay the bills, doing digital marketing and writing copy for a non-profit that specialized in literary advocacy. It was an amazing organization and I was excited to be a part of it, but I was having a hard time focusing on it without thoughts of Zach floating into my head.

I reached into my bag and checked my phone. No texts. My anxiety and bad mood weren't just because of what had happened with Zach at our meeting. As much as I hated to admit it, it bothered me that I hadn't heard from him. I felt pathetic, sitting around waiting for a man to text me, but I couldn't seem to stop. He had my number, so what was the problem? *You didn't even want him to have your number in the first place,* I reminded myself. It was true, but it didn't mean some small part of me wasn't hoping he'd text me, now that he did. I felt myself getting annoyed with my so-called friends again for putting me in this position.

I took a deep breath and tried to relax. It wasn't going to help anything to be mad at them, especially when they thought they were being helpful. Besides, I needed to stop caring about what Zach thought. Despite telling myself this, I reached reflexively into my bag one more time to check my phone. But instead of finding my phone, my fingers brushed against a folded sheet of paper. I pulled it out, unsure what it was, and unfolded it.

Briefly I wondered if it was from Connor. There had been a time, soon after he learned how to write, that Connor would leave me sweet, encouraging notes in my bag, just like I would occasionally leave inside his lunchbox.

But this tidy scrawl wasn't Connor's handwriting.

Roses of crimson
Skies of blue
Nature's beauty has got nothing on you.
Do you know how you affect me?
I don't think you do.
If given the chance, I think I could love you.

My heart gave a little jump as I looked down at the words. I'd never been given a poem like this, there was genuine feeling in these words. Whoever wrote it was sweet and caring, and though I had no idea who it was from, it made me feel all warm and fuzzy inside.

As a single mom, I rarely got to feel special or desired like this, and whoever had written this note definitely brought a little smile to my face.

I wondered who it could possibly be from. There was that guy in my class who kept smiling at me, but he hadn't been anywhere near my bag. At first, I thought it was Kody, just trying to cheer me up, but he swore it wasn't him and besides, it was way too romantic to be from a friend. The sappy part of my brain wondered for the briefest of moments if it could have been Zach, but he was probably the easiest to rule out. This poem was pure emotion. And Zach? He was pure sex. There was no way he was interested in me like that. Plus, I strongly doubted he'd take the risk and put something like this on paper— he could lose his job at the university for getting involved with a student.

Still, it was nice to know that someone was interested. I slipped the poem back in my bag, still smiling. At least one good thing had happened this week.

For the next two hours, I forced myself to focus on work and actually managed to get a few things done. When I was finished, I pulled out my phone to check the time and saw a text from Zach. My stomach did several backflips and my vision went blurry. I wanted to throw the phone across the room, and at the same time could hardly wait to get the text open.

Hey, can we talk?

Yes, I thought, breathing out a sigh of relief, *I am more than ready to move on from this.* Another text came in.

I need to clear the air.

I agree, I started to type in response. I could only assume he was prepared to apologize for how our last meeting went. Before I could hit send, my phone lit up again with a new message.

I'm majorly fucking attracted to you.

My heart felt like it had been ripped out of my chest. I couldn't tell if I was angry, turned on, or some strange and interesting combination of both. I forced myself not to get lost in my desire for Zach, which was becoming increasingly difficult. I wasn't in school to start an affair with my adviser; I was there to focus on writing. I wanted to tell him to get lost, but instead I just stared at my phone, unable to come up with a response. *Damn it, Poppy.*

As if he could read my thoughts, Zach texted again.

What's the worst that could happen?

I bit my lip and looked hard at my phone, as if the perfect response would write itself if I stared at the screen long enough. Of course I wanted to. I wanted nothing more than to run to his house, strip him naked and kiss every inch of his hard inked-up body. My heart sped up at the thought and my mouth went dry. *No.* This wasn't a part of my plan. My plan was to prove that a single mother who got pregnant in high school could still succeed. This whole situation with Zach had already distracted me way more than I wanted it to. After a few seconds I simply said,

I just can't right now.

His response was immediate.

We'll talk about it in person.

I put the phone down for a second and ran my hands through my hair. An in-person conversation might be a good chance to lay down some clear ground rules so that we could keep things professional. But even as I told myself that, I seriously doubted this would work, based on how my other conversations with Zach had gone. I tried to imagine what I would tell him to make my point clear. Did I fess up and tell him about Connor? I was a private person and the thought of sharing so much of my life with him felt like too much. But if I was going to meet with him to discuss this, I needed a solid idea of what I would say before Zach's presence muddled everything.

Just the thought of him sent my mind in a million different directions, and when I was around him... Well, let's just say I'd need a full script written out if I wanted to keep myself on track. Even thinking about being near him made me start to tingle all over, and I could see him flashing that sexy smirk at me already. That smirk made it hard to breathe. It made me think about all of the things I wanted him to do with his mouth. *Shit.* I threw my phone down like it had a disease and fled my room.

One thing I knew for sure. Before I officially decided anything, I'd need some advice. And since my new neighbors knew the whole situation—idiots as they were, I couldn't navigate this alone. I tiptoed out to the living room and kissed the side of Connor's temple. "I'll be right back."

Unwilling to leave Connor more than twenty-feet away, I stepped onto the front porch and knocked on their door, waiting with my hands on my hips.

"Hey." Jodee appeared a moment later, wiping her hands on a kitchen towel. "You didn't have to knock. What's up?"

I motioned to my front door. "I don't want to leave Connor for long, but I need to talk."

Kody appeared behind her in the doorway.

"What's up?" Kody asked raising one brow.

"I'm sorry I was cranky earlier, but I need your help." I paused. "With Zach."

They stepped out onto the porch immediately. I almost laughed. I knew that no matter how much of a bad mood I'd been in, they couldn't resist an opportunity to discuss this situation. It was just too titillating.

"What happened?" Jodee asked, sitting down on the porch swing and tossing her long hair over her shoulder.

I told them about our text conversation and how Zach wanted to meet up in person.

"Are you going to do it?" she asked eagerly.

"I don't know," I sighed. "I don't even know what I'd say."

"This calls for drinks later," Kody announced, standing up. "Want us to come over once the munchkin is in bed?"

Feeling oddly emotional, I swallowed the lump in my throat and nodded. I hadn't had this much of a support network—ever. I lived with my parents all through undergrad, and only moved out at the end of last year into an apartment near campus. My parents had convinced me that no college student would want to room with a chick and her kid, so I hadn't even tried. I'd just stayed sheltered and under their roof—their control—for far too long. And at first, they'd been right. Last year was tough—just me and Connor in a cramped apartment close to campus while I finished my degree and shuffled him back and forth to after-school activities and sports. And as hard as it was relying only on myself, I knew I'd never return to living with them.

It was how we ended up in our half of the duplex this year. We needed a home, Connor deserved a backyard—not just some crash pad because it was the only thing I could afford. So, I'd picked up more hours at my part-time job, and stretched my budget as best as I could.

I never counted on our new home coming with two new friends who were so sweet, understanding and seemed invested in us.

"That would be awesome. Thanks, guys." With that settled, I headed back inside to start dinner.

After two helpings of taco-lasagna, a favorite that Connor and I had invented, he'd taken his bath and was tucked into bed where I read a few chapters in his newest superhero chapter book. That kid loved the bookstore almost as much as I did, and nine times out of ten would prefer a new book to a new toy. Or heck, even a *used* book. Those were pretty awesome, too. I smiled to myself, leaning down to press a kiss to his forehead. We didn't have much, but we had each other, and we had love. And when we needed an escape, we had words to transport us to wherever our imaginations could climb.

"Love you, buddy."

"Love you, Mom." Connor yawned.

I flipped on his night-light and turned off the lamp.

"Night."

By the time I made it halfway down the stairs, I could hear the hushed voices of Kody and Jodee. They were sitting on my couch with a bottle of red wine and three wineglasses on the coffee table in front of them.

"Hey, guys." I plopped down into the armchair across from them, suddenly feeling dead tired.

"Little guy go down okay?" Jodee asked.

I nodded. There was always a certain amount of awe in their voices and expressions when they watched me with Connor. Being a mom while balancing grad school wasn't rocket science, I just did what I needed to do.

Kody uncorked the wine and poured us each a glass. Once we all had a beverage in hand, we dove into the debate.

"So, what should I do?" I asked, taking a small sip of wine.

"He's really hot." Jodee twirled a strand of hair around her finger, thinking. "But he's also your adviser. And I could see feelings developing."

"Forget feelings," Kody interrupted, setting down his

wineglass. "If a guy like that was interested in me I'd have banged his brains out already."

"But we have to worry about school, too. It's not all about fucking," Jodee insisted.

"I'm sorry, but that chemistry you and Zach have— you don't find that every day." Kody was more stone-faced serious than I'd ever seen him.

I sighed, feeling as confused as ever, watching them talk in front of me about this situation as if I wasn't in the room listening. I was the voyeur in their debates over do I or don't I. They both had valid points. I thought about Zach's question. *What's the worst that could happen?* That was exactly what I needed to figure out. We could have sex and it could be amazing. *Oh God*, even just thinking the words was turning me on. I could feel myself running my tongue along his sexy tattoos as he grabbed a handful of my hair. *Fuck.* This was exactly the problem. It was too all-consuming. I forced myself not to think about it.

But I could also get myself in some serious trouble if someone at the university found out. I couldn't jeopardize my future—my son's future—for a few orgasms.

Then, a thought hit me. "You guys, what if sex with

Zach isn't amazing? What if our whole attraction is just anticipation, but the actual thing isn't that great?" This had never occurred to me before, and it horrified me to think of having to go to adviser meetings with him after that. That would suck ass.

"I've been worried about that too...this whole forbidden love thing element can make things seem sexier than they really are," Jodee said quietly, shaking her head and looking at the floor.

"Haven't you two sucked face already? You already know better than anyone that there's chemistry." Kody was to the point, if not delicate.

A lightbulb seemed to go off in Jodee and she nodded, frantically. "He's right. Sex is simply a physical act—anyone can do it and it can be good or bad, but when the right mix of chemistry is involved with the physical-- then the act becomes this explosion of bodies and minds."

Shit. She was right. It really couldn't be bad between us. There was no way it wouldn't be amazing, based on that kiss, but that only made everything more complicated.

I pictured Zach's face, his strong jaw and thick, dark hair, his perfectly toned body. I could still feel his strong hands on my hips as we kissed. That kiss. My face went hot at the thought of it.

Okay, so what if I did "bang his brains out" as Kody put it, and it was amazing. What if we started to develop feelings? Then what would happen? Were students even allowed to date advisers? I could get in trouble with school, and even if I didn't, I certainly wouldn't be taken seriously as a writer. He could lose his job. There was no way that would end well.

I couldn't risk things going wrong. I had worked so hard to get into this program, and now I was thinking of throwing it away over some guy I kissed once? Pull it together, Poppy. Big girl panties from here on out. Adulting sucked, but it was what I needed to do.

"Thanks guys." I lifted my glass toward my friends, acknowledging their advice, but the truth was, the situation had many facets and it wasn't something a couple of glasses of wine and some girl talk would solve.

A little while later I said goodbye to my neighbors and headed to bed. But it turned out climbing under the sheets while still buzzing on wine and thoughts of Zach wasn't a good combination.

Squeezing my eyes closed, I took a deep breath. It shouldn't have mattered how attractive or forward he was. While I found it refreshing to know what he was thinking, our attraction wasn't something we could act on. When I pictured the way his lips quirked up when he read over my work, like he was genuinely pleased, or the way he defended my honor at the coffee shop, dismissing Kody and Jodee once he sensed I was bothered by their visit, made my heart swell a little.

I couldn't believe Kody had called him my hot adviser—right to his face. But there was no denying the man was sexy—he had to know that. Surely he had a functioning mirror at his house. He was six feet of muscled perfection. Just thinking about him got me hot. Realizing sleep was a long way off, and that there was no shame in bringing myself a little relief, I let my hand drift down to the waistband of my pajama pants, and dip under inside of my panties.

I wasn't surprised to find the material already damp and clinging to my sensitive, swollen flesh. With my fingers slick and circling, it only took a few minutes until I was coming undone—gasping for breath with a certain hot adviser's name on my lips.

Chapter Seven

Zach

I could tell before we took our first sips that my mother had already read my aura.

"You're all muddled today. More than usual." She squinted at me, like I was a street sign she was trying to decipher through a rain-soaked windshield.

"Yeah? You see that in my aura?" I asked, with a knowing sigh. This would be a whole lot easier if I just played along. She was like a dog with a bone. If she felt there was something weighing on me, she wouldn't let it go until she'd covered it from every possible angle. But the thing was, I wasn't stressed, not in the way my mother thought I was, at least. I was just more interested in one of my advisees than I had any right to be. We were supposed to be studying literature together. Instead I wanted to take *her* off the shelf, crack her open, and read the *shit* out of her.

And when I'd texted her, and told her as much—radio silence.

My mother cut into my thoughts with a healthy dose

of reality.

"I'm your mother. I don't need to read your aura to see something is on your mind. It's a girl. Please tell me it's a girl," she almost groaned this, excitedly drumming on the table. "Or a boy. I support all sexuality. You know that. I donate to that Human Rights Campaign every month."

"I know, Mom." I smiled, trying not to roll my eyes. She was adorably progressive. "Yes, it's a girl. I may or may not have started," I paused, "*courting* a girl I probably shouldn't be."

"Courting?" she snorted. "Such a poet. You're hitting on her. You want her. You're aching for—"

"Yes, yes, and yes," I interrupted, knowing she'd keep digging if I didn't re-steer the conversation.

"And how's it going?" She smiled brightly, excited by the possibility of me dating again. She'd never really hit it off with my ex. Something about her aura.

"I've hit a wall. She's... sort of a student that I'm advising."

"Sort of? That's like someone saying they are 'sort of

pregnant'...they either are, or they aren't, so which is it?" Her eyebrows raised in that *don't-lie-to-your-mother* way.

"Okay, she is. She's a student. I'm her adviser." This was the first time I was saying it out loud. I felt the weight of the words settle in my chest and into the air between us. Admitting my attraction to Poppy to my mother felt like going to confession.

Good thing Mom was no priest. She threw her hands up in excitement. "If that isn't the sexiest damn thing I have ever heard!"

"Mom, keep it down," I scolded her, but I couldn't hide my chuckle. She was right. It was sexy. So sexy that it had me all kinds of worked up lately. "So, it's obviously kind of complicated."

"Complicated?" My mother placed a hand over her heart in mock distress. "No. It's kismet! It's fate!"

"I wouldn't go that far," I said to the woman notorious for taking *everything* too far. "We're not exactly on the same page. Honestly, I don't know if we're even reading the same book."

"Zachary, look at yourself. What other book could she possibly want to read?" She winked. "You're welcome for the good genes, by the way."

I deflected the compliment easily. "She doesn't want to take it any farther than one kiss we had at a party."

"Well, that's because it was at a *party*. Have you wined-and-dined her? Has my son, the Poet with a capital P, tried to romance her? Or have you just Zach-Attacked the girl?"

"I don't want to know what *that* phrase means," I began with a grimace. "I don't think she'd go for that." It was one of the many things I liked about Poppy. She was strong in her convictions. I doubted she could be romanced into agreement. And I didn't want to bend her to my will. I just wanted her to want me, because I sure as hell wanted her.

My mother narrowed her eyes at me. "Come on, Zach." She scoffed at me.

Okay, maybe I deserved that look of disappointment. I retreated into my coffee, taking another sip.

"Here's what you're going to do," she continued. "One, invite her over for dinner. Two, pour the wine — *keep* pouring the wine. Three, do you still have that chicken picante recipe I sent to you or should I email it…"

"I still have it." It's tucked away in a drawer somewhere along with my dignity. I have never made a woman dinner, and I was not about to start with Poppy. If I were to fuck that up, who knows if my pride would ever recover? Imagining Poppy poking unhappily at an overcooked piece of chicken was not my idea of romance.

"Making dinner on a first date is a little bit of a commitment red flag," I said.

My mother sank back into her chair, assessing me with the eyes of a hawk. "What's that supposed to mean? What is it exactly that you're looking for with this young woman, Zach?"

I paused, taking a sip of my coffee, while my mother continued, on a roll now.

"You have to decide if it's just sex you want or if it's something more. You can't be in between on that point. You can't do that to a woman."

I wanted to argue with her, but I knew my mother was probably thinking about her own failure at relationships. Passion led to sex, which led to pregnancy, which led to a marriage with a swift and inevitable divorce shortly after.

My phone buzzed. I checked the message.

Are we still on for today?

Speak of the devil. It was my father. For years I had a strained relationship with him. He was much older than Mom, nineteen years her senior, and to be honest, I don't think he ever got over the loss of his first wife. My mom was the unlucky rebound he tried to reclaim his happiness with. But one disagreement too many, and my mom packed our bags, vowing we didn't need him anymore.

"Who's that?" My mother peered at my cell. I quickly lifted it out of her view.

Now that I was older, I'd learned to accept my dad's shortcomings and appreciate what he had to offer. Plus, I'd come to realize the old man wasn't going to be around forever.

"Dad," I said. "I've got to run. Thanks for the advice, Mom." I planted a kiss on her forehead before pushing my chair in.

"Mmm-hmmm." She was not convinced. *Don't lie to an aura-reader, Zach. This is gonna bite you in the ass later.*

"You're a good boy, Zachary," she called after me. I looked back over my shoulder to catch a knowing smile. Maybe she knew more than I thought. She usually did.

It took me less than twenty minutes to drive to my dad's apartment from the café. The proximity in which my divorced parents lived was maybe abnormal, but it had never been an issue growing up. My dad was distant, if not physically, then emotionally. It took me most of my adult life to come to terms with the fact that I would have to make the first steps of having any sort of relationship with him.

I knocked on his front door and waited for him to answer. I heard footsteps from inside and then the door was opening to reveal my dad, just how I'd always picture him—gray wool cardigan, button-down shirt, and white hair, parted neatly at the side, looking dapper—even at sixty-nine years old.

"Hey, Dad." I smiled as he reached out and gave my hand a firm shake. "Happy birthday."

"Ah, when you get to be my age, it's no big deal. It's a Monday, you know?"

I nodded. "Happy Monday, then. What would you

like to do today?" I told him I'd pick him up after work and we'd do something to celebrate.

I was guessing Dad would suggest the diner he liked near his house, or maybe just coffee. But he surprised me by allowing a secretive little smile to sneak onto his otherwise stoic face.

"I've got someplace in mind. You're driving."

Once inside my car, he directed me to a quiet little strip mall a few miles down the road.

We parked and got out of the car. I still had no idea where we were going, but I followed him along the sidewalk until he stopped in front of a door to a nail salon with a neon sign promising a "Mani-Pedi for $49!"

"Um?" I paused, sure he had the wrong place.

"Come on, kid. It's my birthday. Let's live a little."

Bells jingled over the door, and the smell of nail polish wafted out to greet us.

"Arthur!" the receptionist sang when she saw my dad, crossing from behind her desk to pull him into a hug.

It was clear my dad was a regular here. *Interesting.*

The place was almost empty—an older woman, probably a retiree like my dad sat in one of the pedicure chairs with her feet soaking in steaming water. A couple of other women sat getting their fingernails polished in vibrant colors.

"This is my son," Dad said, gesturing to me.

"Handsome!" the woman giggled into her hand.

"Thanks," I mumbled, feeling oddly out of place. I was hip. I was with it. I might even be a little metro-sexual with my manscaping and whatnot. But this? This was an entirely new experience for me. Still, I decided to just go with it. *When in Rome and all that shit.*

We were directed to a station in the back and seated side by side while two women emerged from the back of the shop to attend to us.

"You alright there?" Dad asked. Was that a playful smirk I saw?

"Of course."

The longer we sat here, the more I started to assign meaning to our visit here. Maybe it was the writer inside me, but curiosity was a strong motivator, and I needed to piece this together. Dad didn't say it, but I knew what he liked about this place. The petite dark-haired beauty filing his nails and massaging his hands reminded him of his first wife. He'd met her in Cambodia while stationed there with the Army. They'd only been married a couple of years when she was killed in a car accident.

The low hum of conversations around us was spoken in their native dialect. I was confident my dad didn't have a clue what they were saying, but a little smile remained planted across his face, like the sound of chattering women in this faraway language brought him back to a better time in his life.

I smiled at the woman filing my nails, proud that I'd flinched only twice as she trimmed my cuticles with some device that looked like it was straight out of the medieval ages.

As we sat here longer I realized it wasn't just the nostalgia that kept him coming back. It was the level of companionship, however brief, and the human touch that was of comfort to him. He was a single, sixty-nine-year-old man living alone. He probably didn't get touched by another person outside of these occasional visits. It made me feel sad for him.

As I sat there, my thoughts drifted to Poppy, as they often did during a moment of quiet. We needed to talk, to clear the air between us.

I had a weird relationship with love. I wanted it, but I wasn't necessarily looking for it. Honestly, it was probably the thing I wanted most in my life. But wasn't about to go out searching for it like some lovesick puppy. I was waiting for it to find me, if that made any sense. After watching my parents, I knew forcing it was pointless. True love — love that was real and tangible — now, that couldn't be stopped. However elusive it seemed, I knew when the time was right, it would come knocking. Until then, I was going to enjoy all the noncommittal fun I could, knowing that one day I may end up just like my father, having lost his true love and now getting his nails buffed and polished just for a little human contact.

Was this what my life was going to boil down to? That thought was a depressing one.

I thought about what my mom had said. *You have to decide if it's just sex you want or if it's something more. You can't be in the middle. You can't do that to a woman,* her voice rang in my mind.

I knew I wanted Poppy—but I also knew that as her

adviser, she was off-limits. And my plans to move to New York City next year to pursue my writing full-time would be another problem. Hello, rock. Meet hard place.

Chapter Eight

Poppy

You could cut the tension between us with a knife. I'd been a bundle of nerves as I walked into the coffee shop to meet Zach for our meeting, but I needn't have worried. He dove straight into his notes on my poems and had been nothing but professional. We got down to business on my assignment for Dr. Chan, and I felt immensely better and more confident about my piece. I couldn't help but think that perhaps he was trying to make up for the wasted meeting we had where we got nothing done.

Still, I knew we were both aware of the elephant in the room. Zach had texted me that he was "majorly fucking attracted" to me and we weren't talking about it. We never met up to discuss it, mostly because I was too afraid, and my new plan was to pretend it never happened. Which conveniently Zach seemed to be on board with.

"Any questions on the paper Ludwitz assigned this week?" he asked.

I somehow liked that he'd memorized my schedule,

and was taking a vested interest in my performance.

I shook my head. "I haven't actually even started it yet. I thought I'd dig in tonight."

He nodded. "Cool. He comes across as cold, but he's actually a good guy. He is really particular on word count though, so pay attention to that. And let me know if you have questions."

It was nice, actually, to talk about writing with him. I was surprised to find that despite Zach's dirty mouth and tendency to get distracted during our meetings, he was insightful and had a lot of useful notes about my work. This must be the Zach other students got to work with— the cool, smart adviser who was passionate about writing.

As we wrapped up our meeting and walked out of the coffee shop, Zach pointed down the street.

"Do you want to grab a bite?"

I paused, thrown off by the question. He'd been so professional all morning, so what was he trying to do? While there was no rule against students and advisers going out to lunch together, it still felt like it might be taking things too far.

"Come on, Poppy. I see those wheels turning. There's no motive. I'm just hungry, and based on how loudly your stomach was grumbling during our meeting I assumed you were, too."

I couldn't help but laugh and put my hands on my stomach.

"I was hoping you hadn't heard that."

"It was very distracting." He flashed that smirk at me, and my knees went weak. That's not the only thing that was distracting during our meeting. Zach was dressed casually in a blue button up and dark jeans, both of which seemed to have been tailor-made to show off his jaw-dropping body. His dark hair, as always, was the perfect mix of styled and messy. He ran a hand through it at that moment, as if he knew what I was thinking. *Fuck.* Why did it feel like the wind had been knocked out of me every time he did that? I swallowed dryly.

"I guess I do need to eat." I shrugged, trying to sound casual despite my thoughts. *It's just lunch,* I told myself. *And he's right, I'm starving.*

"Cool. If you like sushi, there's a good place that's within walking distance," he said.

I nodded and Zach led the way.

It was a perfect fall day. The leaves were a colorful array of oranges, reds and yellows, the sun was bright and there was a cool breeze. A lot of the local shops had already put up pumpkins and Halloween decorations in anticipation of the holiday even though it was way too early. Still I loved this time of year. It was the perfect weather to snuggle up at home with a book. Or with a hot guy. *Except not Zach. Definitely not Zach.*

As we walked down the street I could feel that same tension from earlier. I knew I needed to say something. I couldn't sit through a whole lunch without at least acknowledging what he'd texted me. My stomach felt like it was full of lead and my hands started shaking so much that I shoved them into my pockets. It was now or never. I stopped mid-stride, "I need to say something."

He turned to me with an amused look, the same look he'd given me at the party when we first met, and the words just fell out of my mouth.

"Look, about what you texted me the other day, I'm sorry, it's not that you're not attractive. You are," I felt my face getting hot, and I hoped I wasn't blushing. *You're the most gorgeous man I've ever seen. Plus you're smart, insightful, a writer ...* I took a deep breath, "But even if I could get past you being my adviser, you've just caught me at a bad time. Post relationship, and all that. I've kind of sworn off men. At least for the time being." *Not to mention I have a seven-year old son I've never told you about ...* I felt like I was struggling to breath, like my stomach was in my throat and my words were almost choking me. That had to be the reason I hadn't brought up Connor yet. Wasn't it?

He was still looking at me with that same expression, then shrugged. "That's fine with me. We'll be friends." I felt relief wash over me, before he added, "With, or without benefits. Up to you."

Just when I thought I was getting through to him. I put my hands on my hips. "No benefits."

"Hmm." The sound was so deep and sexy coming from him. "So, I suppose it's not helpful that I want to fuck you." He put on a mock serious face. "Platonically, of course."

My lady-parts jumped to attention at the word "fuck" coming from his full and very kissable lips, but I forced myself to stay focused.

"No dice. Friends. That's it."

He didn't say anything for a minute, but his eyes moved down my body and I felt my face flush. I was suddenly aware of how my sweater clung to my breasts and how tight my jeans were. My nipples pushed up against my bra as a shiver ran through my spine and down between my legs. I tried to stand as still as possible, hoping Zach wouldn't notice my reaction. When he met my eyes again, he was smirking like he knew exactly what I'd been thinking.

"Fine." He shrugged. "It'll take more work than I thought, but I'll win you over. If not, Kody wants a piece of this fine ass, so there's always that."

I snorted a laugh, unable to stop myself.

"Well I hope you two are very happy together."

"Not that I'm not enjoying having this conversation in the middle of the street but I'm pretty hungry. Can we eat now?" Zach gestured toward the restaurant.

Okay, so we didn't exactly accomplish what I'd hoped but at least I'd made my point. As much as Zach teased me he knew where I stood on this. Despite our attraction, despite our chemistry, despite that kiss ... we had to remain just friends.

Zach led me a few blocks down the street to a sushi restaurant that boasted an all you can eat lunch special. As we looked over the menu my stomach let out another loud grumble. We both started cracking up.

"Luckily this is an all you can eat buffet because it sounds like you haven't eaten in months."

I smiled slyly at him over the menu. "Care to make this interesting?"

He raised an eyebrow and leaned forward. "I'm listening."

"I bet I can eat more sushi than you."

He laughed. "No way, you're tiny. But if you want to make that bet, I'll take it."

It was a little ridiculous, Zach had over a foot of height on me, and countless pounds. But what I lacked for in size, I made up for in gusto. I wasn't going to hold back.

After we'd placed our extravagant orders of four rolls each and handed our menus to the server, I turned to Zach.

"So, what got you into writing?"

"Straight to business. I appreciate that in a woman." He flashed that panty dropping smirk again and I crossed my legs under the table, hoping he wouldn't notice the reaction it gave me down there.

He took a sip of his water and shrugged. "I've just always liked it, since I was a kid. I think it was easier to express myself that way than to say it out loud. And when I got to college and had no idea what I wanted to major in, I just kind of fell into it. I was an English lit major as an undergrad, and then completed my masters here at Vanderburg a couple of years ago in creative writing."

"That's cool. But really…You? Having trouble expressing yourself?" I grinned.

He laughed. "Hard to imagine, right? But I was a shy kid. Obviously, I got over that." He ran a hand through his dark hair.

"After graduation, I got a job offer and stayed on to help in the department. I thought it'd be temporary while I finished my manuscript. I've been here two years now."

"Wow. But it seems like you like it?" I couldn't detect any bitterness in his voice, but I knew that deep down all writers had a secret fantasy about selling their first novel for millions and receiving international accolades. Regardless of what happened with his writing, I found it admirable that he'd stayed on here, coaching writing students to succeed in something he himself was so passionate about.

He nodded. "Yeah, I do actually. But part of me would love to start over somewhere. Do something adventurous like move to New York—pursue my writing career full-time."

"Oh." I wasn't sure what to say. My life and the term adventurous didn't compute.

"What about you? Why poetry?" he asked.

I thought for a moment. I knew the answer, but I wasn't ready to admit all of it to Zach.

I'd always loved to read, but I think having a baby so young pushed me into my hobby more—it was something fun I could still do—it was easy to hold a baby in one arm and a book in the other.

And then my writing was a natural extension from there. I needed a way to express myself, and since I wasn't off running with the cool crowd, or even out socializing much at all, I poured all my thoughts and feelings onto paper. I only had time for short pieces, and poetry came naturally.

"Kind of the same, I guess. I'm not very articulate, but when I'm writing, the emotion kind of just flows out of me. I can push everything else from my brain, all the noise, all the worries and stress and just be in the moment with my words. I love that feeling." I felt myself turning red, and looked down at my hands. "I don't know, it sounds dumb when I say it out loud."

"No, it doesn't. I actually know exactly what you mean." I lifted my eyes and we looked at each other for a moment before we were interrupted by the server delivering our sushi on gleaming white porcelain dishes.

"May the best man win." Zach and I touched our first two pieces of sushi in a mock toast, and started stuffing ourselves.

I chewed and swallowed my first bite. "This is really good. Try the eel." I pointed to my plate, urging him to take a piece.

Zach shook his head. "If I'm going to win, I need to focus on what's on my own plate. Nice try though."

I rolled my eyes.

Usually I felt awkward going out to eat with someone for the first time, but this was surprisingly comfortable.

"So," he said, swallowing a mouthful of spicy tuna. "Since you've sworn off men, should we pick out a woman for you?"

I snorted and put down my chopsticks. "Why don't you help me pick someone out?"

The restaurant was popular and it was completely packed for the lunch special. Zach put a hand to his chin like he was thinking carefully. I should have been looking around as well, but I found myself unable to take my eyes off him. His full lips were turned up in a slight smile, highlighting his already prominent cheekbones. His strong jaw was flecked with scruffy facial hair, making him look effortlessly rugged. When he turned back to me with those heart stopping green eyes, I had to hold back from letting out a little gasp. I quickly looked away, hoping he hadn't noticed me staring.

"What about her?" Zach asked.

His knees brushed mine under the table. But rather than pull away like I expected one of us to do, I couldn't find the will to move away. My heart jumped into my throat, and my pulse began to race. It felt so deliciously guilty to be sitting here with him, discussing all the reasons we couldn't be together—to be actively picking out someone more appropriate for me—and yet lusting after him in this same moment. God, it was practically poetic.

I took a deep breath to calm myself and then looked at who he was pointing at. It was a petite, curvy brunette, about my age.

"Too short," I said automatically. Zach laughed.

"Cutthroat, I like it. But what about her?"

I craned my neck to catch a glimpse of the woman he was pointing at with one of his chopsticks.

I pursed my lips. "Her hair is too blonde. She looks fake."

Zach made a low sound under his breath. "I didn't realize you'd be so hard to please."

"I just want the best." I grinned.

"So, who here is good enough for you?"

I looked around, scanning the crowd, weighing my

options. I pointed at a leggy brunette with curly hair. "She's cute," I said, and continued to stare for a moment, "but a little too tall."

"Well I guess you'd need the gold-standard of snatch if you were really going to consider muff-diving."

I almost choked on the sip of water I was taking, and then I was cracking up. "Zach!" I reprimanded.

"Don't look at me with that tone of voice. You know I'm right."

I rolled my eyes and stuffed another piece of sushi into my mouth. Even if I wouldn't let myself fall for him, I was coming to realize that Zach really was the total package. He was smart, sweet, funny, and the sexiest man I'd ever hung out with. The combination was maddening.

Abandoning his hunt for my new girlfriend, Zach picked up his chopsticks and lifted a piece of smoked salmon to his full lips and totally caught me staring.

Damn.

His mouth twitched in amusement. "You feel things for me, admit it."

I narrowed my eyes. "The only thing you make me

feel is angry. Also, sexually frustrated. But mostly angry."

He laughed, and popped the bite of food into his mouth. "Sure, Poppy. Keep telling yourself that."

I lifted my chopsticks, and when I looked down, I realized I'd finished my entire order.

"Are you tapping out on the sushi eating contest?" I gestured toward his plate, which was still almost half full. He looked from his plate to mine in shock.

"Did you seriously eat more than I did?"

"Never underestimate me." It was my turn to smirk at him.

"You're full of surprises, Poppy. That's what I like about you."

As we left the restaurant, I felt a huge weight lifted off me. Hanging out with Zach felt totally natural. Maybe we could be friends after all and I'd do my damnedest to not focus on the fact that just a look from him could get me wet...

Chapter Nine

Zach

The constant look-but-don't-touch I had with Poppy was fucking torture.

I'd spent each night vowing to think of her as a friend and as a student, and I'd spent each morning hard as a tire iron when I awoke after yet another erotic dream about her.

Last night's fantasy was particularly vivid—Poppy writhed in my bed while I pleasured her with my mouth, my fingers, my cock. The sound of her moaning my name, the sight of her breathless and panting for me. It had seemed so real. Real enough that I woke with a sense of lingering guilt.

At this rate, I was going to have the strongest arm in all of Connecticut without even having to leave my bed to hit the gym. After I made a mental note to switch to lefty if I was afflicted again later that night, my pocket vibrated. I stopped short, digging my phone out and glancing at the screen.

Another message from Poppy. This one said simply:

I see you.

My pulse kicked up as I glanced around, and past the group of students gathered in the grassy area of the quad. I found Poppy's familiar brown eyes staring back at me from one of the very tables I'd been planning to grab.

Beaming, she waved at me and motioned for me to join her. I headed over, trying not to notice the way her cotton shirt clung to her sleek, subtle curves. How many times had I imagined those perfect, teacup breasts in my hands over the past seven days?

I cleared the grit of need from my throat as I approached and pasted a friendly smile on my face.

"Hey. Enjoying the last rays of summer?"

She shrugged and rolled her eyes. "More like procrastinating. Van Buren gave me a massive paper on Chekhov. Not really my style."

"Oh no?" I raised my eyebrows.

"Nope. More of a Tolstoy girl myself."

Any woman who looked like Poppy got my blood pumping—but a woman who looked like Poppy and also enjoyed her Russian literature? That got my dick rock hard.

"Then I look forward to seeing that sarcasm in your writing," I said. "Which is behind, by the way."

She groaned and squeezed her eyes closed. "Slave driver."

"Hey, if you don't want me to look out for your best interest, I'll be happy to let you flounder."

"Who says I'd flounder?" she challenged, one manicured brow raised. "Maybe I've got some tricks up my sleeve."

"I have no doubt about that, but unless they're poems, I'm not interested. Now come on, get up. It's Wednesday. Let's go get some cookies and get to work."

"What does Wednesday have to do with anything?" she asked with a frown, but packed up her books and rose to her feet anyway.

I leaned closer, facing her. "I need you to be completely honest with me," I said, voice quiet and intimate among the chatter surrounding us.

"I've only ever been honest with you," she responded with such honesty. I slid my hand up her shoulders so my thumbs could rest on her collarbone, tucked modestly beneath her scarf. Her hands were hovering at her sides, unsure of themselves, but her eyes stayed latched on mine—so intimately with no hesitation. Her breath caught in her throat, and her gaze strayed down to my lips for just a second before she seemed to catch herself.

"Have you never experienced Warm Cookie Wednesday?"

The question rocked her visibly. She tilted her head and almost looked disappointed by the turn of conversation.

"I have not," she responded with a furrowed brow.

"Well, that, among other things you haven't experienced," I said with a wink, "is a true tragedy. I'm buying." I dropped my hands from her warm, soft skin and stepped back. She visibly leaned forward, craving the contact as much as I still was.

"What if I don't want a cookie?" One of her eyebrows was raised in that combative way that made me want to take her by surprise, dip her back in the crowded café, and steal her breath away with my tongue tangling with hers.

"Do you trust me?" I asked, shoving my hands in my pockets to keep from touching her again. Disarming, professional, distanced. I was back to playing her advisor, not the man with an overwhelming sexual attraction to the devilishly charming woman in line with him.

She nodded, her silky hair falling onto her shoulders as she moved. "I shouldn't."

"Let's go."

Side by side, we walked toward the café and I motioned to the massive line that snaked around the entire building, full of people all waiting for another fresh batch of cookies.

"Whoa, this is no joke," Poppy said, glancing around as we took our place in line.

"Sure isn't," I agreed. "Warm cookies are dead fucking serious. Best day of the week."

"Looks that way," she said with a chuckle.

As we inched closer in line, soon we were almost inside, and close enough to breathe in the scent of warm chocolate, brown sugar, and spice. I glanced down at

Poppy, tucked away at my side, which I liked the sight of way more than I should. Her cheeks were still rosy from the passionate banter of our last conversation. It was getting easier and easier to read this woman, the more time I spent with her. And fuck, I couldn't wait to get to the next chapter.

Five minutes later, we found a quiet spot by the fountain to sit, two giant, oozing cookies in our hands.

"Here goes nothing," she said, the cookie already resting against her perfect lips. I couldn't look away as she took an admirable bite. Then I *really* couldn't look away as her eyelids fluttered closed and the damn sexiest moan I had ever heard rumbled from the back of her throat. She opened her eyes, pupils dilated and fixated directly on mine. A small drop of chocolate rested just beneath her lower lip. I had to take a bite of my own cookie to keep myself from leaning in and licking it away.

"Holy shit," she sighed. "Orgasmic."

She moved closer, and for a second, I just reveled in her nearness. The scent of her skin, the slope of her delicate nose, those lips. "I know." I smirked with a mouthful of perfect, hot pastry.

"How has this not been a part of my life until now?" She looked devastated. The emotions that displayed themselves on this woman's face so purely were absolutely fascinating.

"Maybe it's a message from the universe that you should be trying new things," I offered with a grin. Her eye roll told me that suggestion was a little too on-the-nose. She was still grinning though, so it couldn't have been too much.

"Maybe," she laughed. She held the cookie before her, lifting it up to the light in mock examination and fascination.

"What a pretty sight this is," said a familiar voice. I whipped my head around to see my mother, standing nearby with her usual coffee order in a to-go cup. She smiled broadly at us, eyes twinkling with laughter.

I stood to kiss my mother on the cheek. Poppy stared at us, her smile unsure.

"Not a great time," I said under my breath, trying desperately to get rid of the crazy I knew my mom was about to unleash.

But my mother brushed me off with and easy grin.

"Always a good time, darling." She winked.

"This is my mom," I offered to Poppy, returning to sit beside her.

"Now who do we have here?" She looked Poppy up and down, but Poppy didn't have enough good sense to know she was in the lion's den. Not yet, anyway. Instead, she smiled.

"I'm Poppy. It's nice to meet you, Mrs...."

"Velma, please," my mother interrupted, as she often did. "So lovely to meet you, Poppy. I take it you're the beautiful woman who has my son masturbating through the night?"

Oh, Jesus. I shoved down the urge to throw something and ask her to fetch it far, far away from us.

"Excuse me?" Poppy squeaked.

I could feel the heat rolling off Poppy's cheeks from here. I turned to her. "Just ignore her. She was raised by feral wolves."

Poppy flustered was really damn cute. But she didn't stay flustered for long. She blinked at my mother, her mouth curving into a curious smile.

"You know," my mother continued with the casualness of talking about the weather, "the beautiful girl who has Zach's boxers all tented. Or have you finally transitioned to briefs?" She turned on me. Poppy probably thought the woman was trying to embarrass me. What she didn't know was that the best wing-woman known to man was only giving me a loaded barrel to fire with.

"Don't ruin the surprise, Mom," I responded with a full smile. I could feel the heat of Poppy's cheeks from a foot away.

"Ah, yes, that's for you to know and *you*," she winked at Poppy, "to discover."

Poppy laughed softly, surprisingly charmed by my mother's antics. "I see where your son gets his confidence. I'm envious," she said without a hint of judgment.

That was what I liked about Poppy. She took everything in perfect stride, even my unconventionally honest mother.

"Don't be envious." My mother grasped her arm warmly. "Be open. You'll be much happier."

"Okay, thank you, Mother, as always, for the unsolicited advice. But don't you have something you ought to be doing besides giving me more fodder for my next therapist appointment?" I asked dryly.

She barked out a laugh. "Right. I can take a hint. Just play safely, children."

She clicked away on her sensibly low heels and I turned to Poppy again with a grimace. "I honest to God don't know what to say about that except that I am so, so sorry. All I can say is that she is a really good person and the rest makes up for…that."

She shook her head, the flush finally starting to recede, leaving behind a glow and a half-smile. "It's really okay. It was actually pretty informative."

I raised my eyebrows. "How so? Aside from informing you that my mother is a nutcase with no boundaries?"

"Well, now I see where you get it from. You know, your..." She glanced around to make sure we weren't being overheard and added, "Your sexual openness."

Now it was my turn to laugh. "If that's what you want to call it. I'd like to think I have a little more tact than my mother, though."

"I'm sure you would like to think that," Poppy teased.

But there was no question that, for the next few minutes as we finished our food, the sexual tension between us had only amped higher. Out of the corner of my eye, I could see her eyeing me speculatively, wondering if it was true. Maybe even imagining me stroking my cock while thinking of her. And damned if the distance between us didn't slowly diminish, until her arm was brushing mine and our knees touched beneath the table.

Zach, one.

Psycho cockblock mom, zero.

"What's on your mind? You have a weird look on your face," she said.

I shook my head. "Just thinking."

"About what?"

"What kind of girl we need to find you," I said with a grin.

"Oh, that's right. Because I've given up on guys and you think the—what did you call it? The Gold Standard of

Snatch can be found here on this campus?"

I eyed her, half tempted to tell her that the gold standard had already been set and she was it, but thought better of it and closed my mouth. "Can't hurt to look, right? I just need to know what to keep my eyes peeled for. Given it any more thought?"

She rolled her eyes. "You really aren't going to let this go, huh?"

"My quest to find you everlasting happiness with the woman of your dreams?" I shook my head curtly. "Nope. So let's hear it."

"Your mom seems like a good option." She waggled her eyebrows and I let out a groan and raised my milk glass to her.

"Touché. That was one hell of a burn."

"Oh, no, I'm serious. She might be the one," she teased.

"So, you're looking for someone who will offer you a lifetime of telling people when and where you've had sex with them?"

"She wouldn't do that to her partner, right?" Poppy

asked, her eyes widening again.

"Think again. She's ruined many a Christmas with stories of her exploits."

"Dear Lord."

"You're not kidding," I chuckled.

"Fine, so, not your mom," she conceded. "But, you know, someone funny like her."

"Funny is good. Smart is better," I agreed.

"Smart." She nodded. "Always good to be with someone smart."

"Big boobs?" I countered.

"Definitely not. Intimidating." Poppy winced.

"I'm not much of a boob man, either." I admitted with a nod, using every drop of my self-discipline not to even glance at the outline of her pert breasts beneath her shirt again.

"Ah." Poppy's gaze latched onto mine. "So, we're trolling for a girl for you as well?"

"Hey, I'm always open for business." I said the words, but I didn't mean them. There was only one woman I was interested in. No one else mattered.

From Poppy's loose ponytail, several strands of hair had escaped, and I wished I could reach out and tuck them behind her ear.

"Yeah, so your mom mentioned." Poppy pushed the hair from her face, messing with it twice before finally getting it fixed.

Our words might have been casual, playful, but the tension between us had never felt higher.

"You think you're so funny, don't you?" I asked.

"I know I'm funny," she shot back. "But what else is going on the dating profile. She's smart and funny with reasonable breasts. If that was all, you'd be married with five kids by now."

"Okay, well, I'd need to be with someone who loved writing and books the way I do."

"You don't want to be talking Chaucer while she's watching TMZ?" Poppy raised her eyebrows. "Now you're just being picky."

"She can watch whatever she wants, she just also needs to know how to read, too," I amended.

"Literate. That's a tough one to come by." She laughed, and I took a bite of my cookie.

When I finished chewing, I added, "I thought you wanted to help me?"

"Technically, you wanted to help me. I'm just along for the ride at this point."

"Fine, then, nothing else."

"Oh, come on. Tell me," she urged.

"There really isn't." I shrugged. "I mean, it would be nice to find someone who challenges me. And I'd like to find someone who is sexually adventurous, but those are bonus items."

"Sexually adventurous?" she repeated, her voice sounding slightly huskier than it had only moments before. Husky in a way that had my blood pumping south again.

"Maybe adventurous isn't the word. But I can't deal with a prude. I want someone who isn't just going to lay there and make the occasional noise, you know?" I shrugged. "I'm not interested in a lukewarm sex life. It's way too important."

Poppy blinked and the pretty blush that had coated her cheeks before returned. "Well, I can certainly understand that. But no whips and chains?"

I grinned, momentarily surprised and charmed by her candor. "I mean, I'm open to whips and chains. To be honest, I'm open to most things. I never say never. Pleasure is all too fleeting in this world."

"I'll be sure to add all that to your Okay Cupid profile," Poppy said, pressing a palm to one of her rosy cheeks. "Anyway, I should probably be getting to this damned paper."

"Right." I nodded, ignoring the twinge of disappointment. This conversation was just heating up.

She got up to leave, then turned on her heel and walked back toward me. "Oh, shoot, before I go."

"What's up?"

She zipped open her backpack and pulled out an all-too-familiar looking sheet of paper, now soft and worn at the edges from her fingers. My stomach kicked up into my throat, and sweat dotted my palms.

"I have some homework for you, too," she said.

"That's not how this arrangement works," I countered. "I *give* the homework. I don't *get* the homework." It wasn't entirely accurate, I only mentored her work, but it got my point across.

She rolled her eyes but handed the paper to me all the same. I looked at it, momentarily studying my own words, my own handwriting, wondering if she knew. If now was the moment she was going to call me out, to put a stop to this.

"What's this?" I asked casually, though my blood thundered in my ears.

"A poem," she responded. "Handwritten. I found it in my backpack the other day. I think I have a secret admirer." She looked at me with the innocence of a fucking baby deer. "Do you have any idea who it could be? He writes so beautifully."

"There's any number of talented poets in the program. How do you know it's a man?"

"The language is male."

I wasn't sure what to say to that, but luckily Poppy continued.

"When you're going over assignments, do you think

you could keep your eyes peeled for that handwriting? I don't want to lead anyone on but it's…I don't know. I just want to know who it is."

"Right." I nodded. "Of course, I can do that."

I took a look down at the words I'd written and stuffed into her bag during our sushi date. I wondered when she had found this one. I also wondered how she could possibly be so clueless about the fact it was from me.

"Thanks, Zach." She beamed again. "Talk to you soon."

And just like that, she swiveled back around and headed out across campus.

Still, as she walked away?

As I thought about all the things I'd listed about the kind of woman I wanted to fall in love with?

I was coming to realize, there was a lot more between us than the possibility of swapping bodily fluids, and that made this game incredibly dangerous and twice as stupid.

Poppy, sweet Poppy. Dangerous Poppy. She was pure fire. And I could not have been any more willing to throw myself headlong into the flames.

Chapter Ten

Poppy

"You guys are coming with us," Kody informed me and Connor, leaning on the doorframe to our dining room. He was wearing black skinny jeans and a purple sweater with a large apple printed on the front. Two apple earrings dangled from his ears and sparkled in the sunlight as he walked across the room to the table where Connor and I were camped out—me with a textbook and him a worksheet containing that week's spelling words.

"Where to?" I asked, fighting to keep the annoyance out of my voice. I had three loads of laundry to fold, and dinner to make, and I was supposed to read forty pages of this book before class tomorrow and come prepared to discuss it. Right now, the only thing I felt prepared to discuss was how horribly dry it was.

"Jodee and I are going apple picking and you two have to come." Kody crossed his arms and looked at me. "All you do is mom, work, and write." For emphasis, he gestured around the room to the piles of books, stacks of papers, and Connor's half-assembled science project.

I pushed back my chair and rose to my feet. "First, mom is not a verb. Second, that's kind of my life." Hard work was in my genes. It'd been bred into me from the time I was born. Call me crazy, but I never wanted to feel unprepared for my next class, or like I hadn't done my best work. I had a child to provide for—I wasn't allowed to half-ass it.

Kody leaned against the side of the table.

"I need to finish the assigned reading," I told him as I opened the window to gauge the temperature outside.

"I'll fill you in on the basics on the way," he offered.

"You read it?"

He shook his head. "No one does the assigned reading. I skimmed."

I shut the window with a little shiver, there was a chill in the air, wrapping my arms around myself. The truth was, I could sit here for the next hour and read every word, but I knew I'd never absorb it.

"Please Mom, can we go? Please?" Connor's sweet honey-colored gaze looked up at mine, and it was all the reassurance that I needed. A little break and some afternoon sunshine might do us some good.

"Okay, you win, we'll go apple picking with you."

Kody grinned and strode from the room. His spirit was infectious, and he had a point, debating the topics in the assigned reading wasn't part of our grade—the papers were.

I volunteered to drive because it always helped me relax. Plus, Connor's booster seat was a pain to move, and then I could control the radio too, so that nothing inappropriate got played for little ears. Not that Kody and Jodee would do that. They were very sweet and respectful of Connor. We sat in the car waiting for Jodee, who always took forever to get ready. She finally ran out to meet us at the car. She was also wearing a sweater with an apple pattern.

"Why didn't I get the memo about these apple sweaters?" I asked, looking down at my plain black cable knit.

Kody shrugged.

It was another little reminder that my life was about working, school, and raising my son. I didn't have time for their bar-hopping or the thrift-store hunting excursions they favored. And that was perfectly fine with me. I'd made my peace a long time ago that there were things I was going to miss out on. Okay, that was a lie—but it was *mostly* fine with me. There were only a handful of times when my desires for something I couldn't have actually bothered me. Zach was one of those instances.

But I refused to let this afternoon be about Zach— the academic adviser I wanted to ride like a rodeo bull. He didn't even know about Connor, and even though that bothered me, on another strange level—part of me liked that too. I liked that to him I was just a normal grad student, a girl he was attracted to. It was nice not to feel like a mom for five seconds. I knew I would tell him eventually, but I wasn't sure when that might be. We didn't have to share every intimate, personal thing with each other, did we?

We pulled up to the little farm stand, and followed the gravel road around to the parking lot. Connor excitedly led the way, bounding up the trails and pointing out the giant bounce house at the other end of the farm.

We took our time, picking apples and then selected four huge pumpkins. After we paid, we sat on stumps drinking cider from plastic cups, while Connor jumped inside the bounce house.

"It seems so far away but I know it's going to go so quickly," Jodee said, sipping her cider. "What do you think you want to do after graduation?"

"I want to write, but I also want to keep doing content creation on the side for extra money," I told her, wrapping my wool scarf tighter around my neck. "If I work hard at my part-time job now, I could get hired full-time later."

Kody was nodding. "It's so hard to make a living as a writer. I think I want to teach."

I pictured Kody strutting around the front of a classroom, using a pointer for dramatic effect. Jodee and I grinned at each other, and I could tell she was picturing a similar scenario.

"I think you'd be good at that," she laughed.

"I'm also hoping to publish a book of poems within a year of graduation," I said. I'd been working feverishly trying to finish enough poems to have a collection by the time I graduated. Even then, I'd still need to worry about finding an agent.

Growing up, some of my favorite moments were reading from Shel Silverstein's book of poems, *A Light in the Attic*. It would be a dream come true to hold a book of my own poetry in my hands, to know that people around the world were reading my words.

"Always the overachiever," Jodee smiled.

"You should talk," I said, playfully poking her arm. She already knew she wanted to work in publishing when she graduated. She was the Assistant Editor of our school's literary journal, on track to becoming Editor in her second year.

When Connor was finished inside the bounce house, out he slid, running over to me excitedly.

"Thanks Mom."

I ruffled his sweaty hair and pressed a kiss to his forehead. "Love you buddy."

As we headed back to my car, hauling our apples and pumpkins into my trunk, my phone vibrated. My heart sped up. It was Zach.

I found the perfect woman for you.

I grinned, remembering our conversation from the other day.

Interesting. Double date?

He texted back immediately.

Just tell me when and where.

On the ride home I was quiet, distracted by thoughts of Zach. I needed to keep my focus, especially if I wanted to maintain my sanity. But he always found a way to sneak into my head. He was so incredibly distracting, and it didn't help that every time I thought of him my body started to tingle and I got all hot and bothered between my legs. I shook my head, hoping I could shake out the memory of Zach with his shirt sleeves rolled up, tattoos and muscular forearms revealed. *Fuck.* This was ridiculous. I seriously needed to get a vibrator before I totally lost my mind over this guy.

* * *

"There's my brown-eyed girl," Christopher sang, strutting toward me at the front of the salon.

As much as I loved getting my hair done—what girl didn't? Someone else to shampoo and blow dry your hair was worth its weight in gold. I loved spending time with my stylist too. "Hey Chris," I greeted him, returning his air kisses.

Today he was dressed in a pair of skin-tight black

jeans, combat boots, and a Hello Kitty t-shirt. A little ironic, the writer in me noted.

"You changed your hair," I commented following him back to his station.

After placing my purse on the shelf, I took a seat in the black leather styling chair, and admired his new look.

Christopher changed his hair as often as I changed my outfits. Okay, not really, but every time I came in, it was different.

It was grown out on top and dyed pink with the underneath shaved this time.

"You like it?" He looked straight ahead into the mirror, ruffling it with his fingers.

"It's super cute on you."

"José likes it too." He laughed like it was some inside joke between them.

José was his boyfriend of three years. I was here at the salon one day when José came and dropped off Christopher's lunch. I wasn't sure why it surprised me that his other half was so masculine—a ruggedly handsome, in an unkempt sort of way, construction worker no less.

Maybe because Christopher wore makeup and was just as comfortable in leggings and a tunic as he was in jeans. But they made such an odd couple, it was endearing. What they had was clearly true love and acceptance, and I wasn't about to knock it. We should all be so lucky.

"So, what are you thinking? The usual?" he asked.

I nodded. My tastes were boring compared to his, but Christopher never made me feel that way. Instead he was encouraging, using words like classic and timeless to describe my sense of style.

"The usual," I confirmed. We kept my long tresses shaped with a few simple layers to allow for some movement, and added a color gloss to the whole thing since my dark brown hair tended to go dull.

While we washed and trimmed and blow-dried, I brought him up to speed on my life, like my break-up with Jason, and all the latest with Connor. Christopher was supportive of the breakup, and admitted that I never seemed quite happy when I was with Jason.

We chatted casually as he worked on updating my hair, and we had no problem enjoying stretches of comfortable silence too. I'd been coming to Christopher for a couple of years now, and so being in his chair was relaxing for me.

"What else is new? You like your graduate program as much as you thought you would?"

I nodded, my mind immediately conjuring an image of Zach, his shirt-sleeves rolled up, looking at me over the rim of his paper coffee cup.

"Yeah." I swallowed, uneasily.

Christopher laughed, the sound light and musical. "What was that look for?"

I rolled my eyes. "It's just ... my program adviser. His name is Zach, and ..."

"And you like him." Christopher smiled devilishly. "Is he yummy?"

I cleared my throat. I was about to deny it, to lie and avoid and try and hide from the truth. But damn it, Zach was yummy. I just hated that fact.

"I sort of... kissed him."

Christopher's eyes went wide. He knew just how out of character that was for me. I was a rule-follower through and through.

"It was the weekend before classes started," I explained. "We were at the same party. My new neighbor had dragged me there to distract me from the breakup, and Zach happened to be there, as a chaperone for a friend's younger brother." I didn't tell him the part about asking Zach to pretend to be my date, because it didn't feel relevant. Nothing between us was pretend. Even from that first night. "We just sort of clicked you know, and then he kissed me and it was... everything."

"Wow. That's awesome, girl."

I shook my head, admiring the way my hair now finished, fell in loose waves around my shoulders. "It's not that simple. I mean, I'm working with him in a professional, academic capacity." I wasn't sure who I was trying to convince, him or me.

Christopher spritzed my tresses with a bit of hairspray and shrugged his shoulders. "When you find someone you click with, don't fuck with the universe's plans. That's all I know. If you like him, you like him. I say go for it."

I rose from his chair, my stomach unsettled. Why was this such a non-issue for all the gay men in my life?

Maybe they were just less-complicated, they didn't see the issue with all the same hang-ups and caution tape that I did. Was it possible that everyone was right? That I needed to throw caution to the wind and see where my attraction to Zach might lead?

Chapter Eleven

Zach

When the end of yet another long week finally arrived, I headed home with a briefcase full of half-finished outlines, and poems to review.

Not that I could focus on any of it.

With Poppy around—and even when she wasn't—I spent my time drifting between a sad attempt at concentrating on my work and fantasizing about calling her into my office just to bend her pliable body over my desk and take her in every way I'd imagined.

And so far?

I'd done a lot of imagining.

Every time I found a free moment, it felt like she was the only thing to fill my mind. When I read, I compared the prose to her own work. When I walked down the street, every woman I saw was held in contrast to her.

And even that wouldn't be so bad if it weren't for the constant stream of fantasies that ran through my head. No longer was she satisfied with taking over my dreams. Now the time of day didn't matter. All I could think about was how pretty, how special, how smart she was.

Even thinking of her now, my dick twitched with the need to satisfy the ache for her, but I ignored it, focusing instead on opening my front door and making my way to my office. I'd practically rubbed myself raw just thinking about this woman, but I couldn't allow myself to go down that path tonight.

I had work to do and I was going to do it.

Striding past the foyer, I made my way to my home office and breathed in the scent of fresh paint and sawdust that now always reminded me of home.

Lately, I hadn't had much time to work on it, but over the summer I'd spent my time renovating my house, bringing it back to the glory days of what it had looked like when it had first been built.

Every detail took time—from sanding the moldings to matching the spindles on the staircase until they were exactly like what might have been there two centuries ago.

I was proud of it all, but none so much as my office. With its wide, built-in bookshelves and its stone fireplace, it was the kind of place every literary person dreamed of writing in.

With rows upon rows of thick, leather-bound books lining the walls and a crackling fireplace as the soundtrack, it was the sort of space that was designed to make a person think brilliant thoughts.

Pulling out my rolling leather desk chair, I sat down and set my briefcase on my desk, heaving the mass of papers onto the lacquered wooden surface.

Silently, I glanced at the cold, empty fireplace, but then a paper fell onto the floor and I bent down to pick it up, seeing almost instantly that it was one of Poppy's latest pieces.

The poem was beautiful and short, describing the seasons as two lovers—summer with a fiery temper and thrilling, colorful thrushes, and fall as her lover, staid and secure. Maturing. But it's only when summer left completely that everything died away into winter's chilled, frozen grip and the lovers are reunited, fresh and new as spring blossoms.

It wasn't my genre, it wasn't even my style, but there was no denying the beauty of her work. She thought in ways I couldn't, and that—almost more than anything else—was what intrigued me about her.

I turned to my laptop and clicked to open my latest manuscript, studying the chilliness in my own work. I wondered what Poppy might think of this if she saw it—if she would wish there was more romance and movement and life in my words like there always was in her poetry.

Slowly, I re-read my opening paragraph, then deleted it, trying my best to channel the passion and longing and fierce determination that Poppy might have. And when I read it over again? There was no doubt it was more engaging than the original.

Fuck.

I ran a hand through my hair and sighed. I was supposed to be the teacher, and she the student. It was just this damn distraction, the notion of her that made me second-guess everything I thought I knew. This was bad. The more she infiltrated my life, the worse off I'd be. Especially when I wasn't even sure I was going to be here next year.

Running a hand through my hair, I considered my options. Clearly, I wasn't going to be able to work tonight, not when she was so on the forefront of my mind. I could, maybe, continue the work on my house, but I worried that the silence and the solidarity would only allow my mind to wander back to thoughts of her.

What she might look like sitting in my living room, snuggled close as we watched TV. Or better yet, what she might look like straddled on top of me on that sofa, her hips rolling into me as I—

Another aching throb surged between my thighs and I adjusted myself again.

I couldn't afford to be left to my own devices.

Which, then, only left one option.

Getting the fuck out of this house.

Picking up my cell phone, I shot out a group text to a bunch of buddies to join me at the bar down the street from my house.

Sliding on my light fall jacket, I headed down the block, trying to focus on what autumn brew I'd try tonight instead of how badly I wanted to call Poppy and invite her along too. The idea of spending time with her outside of a school agenda, with the chance to discuss poetry to learn more of her fears, her dreams was a sharp pulse of desire. But I couldn't think of any logical reason that an adviser would have for inviting a student out to a bar.

After a few minutes, the phone in my pocket let off half a dozen dings, all of which were messages from my friends letting me know whether or not they could make it. Dave was out of town with his girlfriend. Brandon was spending a night at home with his wife. Dean was looking after his baby while his wife went out.

All the unfortunate side effects of aging—friends who couldn't leave to head to the bar at the drop of a hat. Still, a few of my friends did say they were down for a beer, so when I walked through the fingerprint-smudged glass doors of The Local, I sidled up to the bar and ordered a few shots along with my beer.

Everything came in short order, and I sipped my beer, glancing at the baseball game on the television before taking one of the shots in front of me and downing it.

The sweet rush of heat coursed down my throat and I hissed my relief just as I felt a warm, huge hand clap down on my shoulder.

"Not messing around tonight, huh?" Tony, a professor in the math department, took the seat beside me and grabbed a shot, sliding the third and last glass toward me.

"To the end of another school week," Tony said, lifting his tiny glass and I clinked it against my own before shooting it back and letting out another low groan of satisfaction.

"How was your week?" I asked, more out of politeness than interest.

"It was a week," Tony said. "You?"

"Just about the same." I sighed, taking another sip of my beer. "Just wanted to get out and clear my head."

"Don't blame you there. These damn budget cuts have been insane." Tony shrugged before ordering from the bored looking bartender. "I'll tell you when I started here thirty years ago, things were different. The students were less entitled, the staff had more respect. It was a different world."

"I bet," I said.

Tony shook his head. "What I wouldn't give to get

that time back. It was like the wild west compared to today when they micromanage everything you do."

I nodded. "I wouldn't know."

Silence fell between us and I took another sip of my beer as I considered Tony's words. He had a point, but more than that, there was something I needed to know. Something everyone talked about, but I doubted anyone addressed with him directly.

"Your wife used to be one of your students, right?" I asked.

He blinked. "Oh, uh, yeah. See, that was way back in the day. Nobody even thought twice about it back then. Now they look at me like...well, you know." Tony rolled his eyes. "It was my second year here and she was a master's student. We were only a few years apart. Not so strange."

"You think?" I asked.

"Not back then, no. Now, though..." Tony raised his eyebrows. "Why do you ask?"

I feigned my best nonchalant look. "Just curious, I guess."

A few more of our buddies arrived and I ordered yet another round of shots as we fell into a discussion about baseball, football, and educational pedagogies. For us, it was a pretty typical night, but even surrounded by my closest friends, I couldn't seem to stop thinking about Poppy.

Like Tony said, it was wrong to date her now. People wouldn't look on it kindly even if we did happen to get away with it.

Then, of course, there was Poppy herself to consider, too. Poppy and her damned insistence on swearing off men—no matter how much bullshit that was.

She wasn't done with men. I'd felt it in her kiss that night at the party, could see it in her eyes every time she looked at me. She had to know she didn't mean it.

And still…she was holding to those boundaries as best she could. Yet another thing I liked about her.

"Another shot?" One of the guys nudged me and I took the glass without thinking, toasting along with them before downing yet another round.

"You still here?" Danny, another friend from the science department, asked. "You look out of it."

Vaguely, I nodded. "Yeah, yeah, I'm here. I just...I need a minute."

Silently, I slid from my stool and realized a little too suddenly that walking was easier said than done. Straightening, I made for the door again and pushed my way into the crisp, night air.

Rubbing my hands over my arms, I psyched myself up and considered my options one last time.

Poppy was a student.

Poppy wasn't interested in dating.

And fuck if Poppy wasn't also everything I'd ever wanted in a woman.

Could I really let her slip away? All for some false excuse that didn't ring true to either of us?

Quickly, I shoved my hand into my pocket and dialed the number I'd been itching to contact all night—hell, all week—long.

Then her musical voice sounded over the line. "Hello?"

"Poppy?" I said.

"Zach," she said, her voice warming. "Hey."

"Hey. Would you like to attend a reading with me?"

There was a brief pause, and I wasn't sure what she'd say. But when she spoke again, I could tell she was smiling.

"I would love that, actually."

What could be more innocent than a poetry reading?

Chapter Twelve

Poppy

The phone call from Zach last night was unexpected, and our plans for later were threatening to take over everything else. But right now, I needed to focus.

I clicked off the radio in my car, and focused on the road instead. I took a deep breath in and let it out, slowly going over what I wanted to say. I'd rehearsed countless times this morning, but I still felt unprepared. I had a fear of public speaking, and even though this was just a group of seven-year-olds, I couldn't help but get butterflies in my stomach at the thought of presenting in front of the class.

When I arrived, the teacher opened the classroom door and beckoned me inside. Connor was seated in the front row and I couldn't help but smile at the sight of him with his hair neatly parted on the side and the adorable gap between his front teeth. I gave him a little wave and he grinned at me and waved back. His eyes sparkled on mine, calming me, and I smiled wider when I saw he was wearing his astronaut t-shirt, which he only took off when

I forced him to. He'd asked me to come to his class to present about being a writer for career day and I was touched that he'd asked me over my parents. I mean, technically I didn't even have a career. My dad would have made a better choice—he was a retired manufacturing manager. But Connor had asked me, and so here I was, ready to present about being a writer.

Even though Connor was only seven, he was pretty much my best friend. He had such a big heart and always made me laugh, even on my worst days. He was obsessed with becoming an astronaut and I wanted to do everything I could to encourage him. My parents were notorious dream crushers; they'd wanted me to have a "normal" major so I could get a steady job straight after college. They'd never believed in my writing and it had caused so many fights that things were strained between us. I knew I could succeed as a writer and I wanted to prove it not only to them, but to Connor, so that he knew it was possible to achieve your dreams. I knew my parents were going to do the same thing to him that they did to me and try to force him into a mediocre life, but he loved math and science and I knew he could do whatever he put his mind to.

The teacher introduced me, and I launched into my speech about writing. And soon, my fifteen minutes were up and I was fielding questions from the class with a big smile. All the tension I'd felt earlier had disappeared. It turned out, when you were discussing something you were passionate about, even public speaking could be easy.

After the presentation I met Connor in the hallway, where he gave me a big hug.

"That was awesome, Mom!"

I pressed a kiss to his forehead. My son affirming that I had done a good job made me feel oddly sentimental and weepy. Blinking back the tears I felt stirring, I hugged my son again.

"So, did you decide what you want to be for Halloween?" I had promised to take him to the store to pick out a costume after school.

"An astronaut," he said, proudly with a little smirk.

Of course. It was the same thing he'd been every year since he was four.

"Seriously, Connor, you can become anything you want. No matter what anyone says, or how hard it is, no matter the obstacles that might be in your way, you get to choose the life *you* want."

"Just like you," he said.

"Exactly." I grabbed both of his hands and gave them a little squeeze. I could tell he didn't fully know what I meant, but I hoped some of what I'd said would stay with him as he got older and his goals started to seem more and more difficult to achieve.

I hugged him again, squeezing tight, and sent him back to class. As I walked out to my car I couldn't help but wonder if I was following my own advice. I was going after my dream of becoming a full-time writer, against all the obstacles that were in my way, but what about other parts of my life? I thought about Zach. Did I have to sacrifice relationships so I could succeed in my career? For now, at least, I couldn't risk messing up, especially when there was so much riding on my success.

* * *

I checked myself in the mirror one more time, nerves making my hand shake slightly as I lifted a hand to bobby pin a stray hair from my face. *Why am I even nervous?* I had been alone with Zach a handful of times, but this felt different. We'd never gone out of our way to meet up outside of school like this. *It's just a reading.* I told myself, which was basically like school. Plus, I'd been dying to hear Ariel Elderson read ever since Zach had introduced me to her work earlier in the semester, so when he'd invited me to this event I didn't hesitate to say yes.

After picking out his Halloween costume, I'd dropped Connor off at my parents' house for the evening. They lived nearby and still kept Connor overnight one or two nights a month. My parents loved it, Connor loved it, and despite how I felt about it— I needed the help. The truth was, sometimes having help made me feel guilty, like I needed to be doing more or that I shouldn't need so much help, but it was nice being able to count on them when I had a late night of schoolwork or just wanted to do something socially with friends. I'd missed so much of that having a baby in high school.

I applied mascara and a touch of eye shadow. I put on red lipstick, then wiped it off. *Be casual,* I told myself. I gave myself another once over, adjusting my fitted green turtleneck and black skinny jeans. Once I was satisfied I slipped into my favorite pair of black boots and headed downtown.

The reading was being held at Book Soup, a

bookstore near the university. It had a funky, eclectic vibe and the walls were covered floor to ceiling with bookshelves. It was the best place near campus for writing events, and an even better place for finding cheap, used books. Zach was waiting for me out front, and as I approached I realized I had mostly seen him in his work clothes. I had to admit, the sight of him in a casual black jacket, dark jeans and brown lace-up boots was havoc on my libido.

"Shall we?" He gestured inside. Even after all this time, his smile still managed to turn my legs to molasses.

"Absolutely," I said, letting him guide me inside the warm book shop.

As we took our seats near the front, I turned toward Zach.

"Thank you so much for inviting me, you have no idea how obsessed I am with her poetry."

"I knew you'd like her." Zach smirked at me. "I'm *such* a good adviser," he said in a mock serious tone.

I punched him playfully on the shoulder.

"Don't get too cocky. I still don't understand who

put you in charge."

He opened his mouth, no doubt to come back with a playful remark, when Ariel walked onstage. Her words were beautiful, and so was she. She had long, black braids and wore thick glasses with white frames and a floor length black dress. Her poems were so moving I felt myself tearing up at one point, quickly wiping them away so Zach wouldn't notice.

"That was amazing," I said quietly when she'd finished. Zach quickly stood up and grabbed my hand. My heart went into sudden overdrive at the feeling of his hand on mine.

"Come on," he said, pulling me over toward where Ariel was standing.

"What are you—" I started to say, when Ariel turned toward us and a smile spread across her face.

"Zach," she said, going in for a hug. I stood watching with my mouth hanging open. They knew each other?

"Amazing as always," Zach said to her, then turned to me with a mischievous look in his eyes. "And this is Poppy. She's a huge fan."

Ariel turned with a swing of her long braids. "Hi,

Poppy, it's so nice of you to come."

I could feel my face burning as I reached out a hand, still in shock, and stammered out a hello. After Zach and Ariel said goodbye, I turned to Zach with my mouth gaping.

"You knew her this whole time?"

"We went to undergrad together. She was in some of my classes." He was grinning, and I knew he was relishing how shocked I was.

"So, should we grab dinner? I know how you love to eat," he said, as if nothing interesting had just happened.

I was still trying to recover from the surprise as we headed out into the chilly night. He was right, I was starving.

"I know a place over here." He gestured down the street.

"If your taste in restaurants is anything like your taste in poets, I'm in."

I shivered as we walked; the night had gotten colder than I'd expected and I hadn't brought a jacket. Zach glanced at me and without a word pulled off his jacket and put it around my shoulders. I was about to protest when I stopped myself. *He's just being nice.* When had I become so cynical?

As he led me toward the restaurant, Zach put his hand on my lower back. It was such a small, innocent gesture, but I felt the heat and energy from his touch as if it were burning right through my layers of clothing.

The restaurant was a small Italian place with white table cloths and small, glowing candles that made it feel cozy. The kitchen was open, and the cooks shouted to each other while the fire from the stoves blazed in front of them. Zach waved to a few of the staff.

"How do you seem to know everyone?" I asked, laughing after our waiter pulled Zach into a quick embrace.

"I come here a lot," he said, shrugging casually.

Our server brought over two glasses of red wine, and after he left, Zach raised his glass to me.

"To getting to know you better."

His sensual words washed over me, and I could no longer deny the effect Zach had on me was dizzying.

We clinked glasses and took a sip. The wine was smooth and rich. It was delicious.

Our server appeared again, and I ordered something I couldn't pronounce that was made with thick noodles and a wild mushroom ragù.

This entire evening had already been more than I'd expected. He could really be a gentleman when he wanted to. "Thank you for your thoughts on my paper for Dr. Chan."

Zach glanced up at me, setting his wineglass down on the table. "How'd it turn out?"

"She was impressed by my piece—she said the parallel I drew between daybreak and infancy was fresh and unique."

"You're a brilliant writer, Poppy." There was no hesitancy, no playfulness to his tone—his compliment was genuine and sincere, and it meant more than I ever expected.

"So, you're still thinking New York?" The moment the question was out of my mouth, I wanted to stuff it back in. I settled for taking another sip of my wine. I hated that I was so obvious—that my interest in his plans next year could be construed as my interest in him—but wasn't that why I was asking?

"That's the plan," he said, voice low. "What about you? Thoughts on graduation, or where you'll end up?"

It was a long way off. I'd just started a two-year program, and even though I loved making plans and setting goals for the future, I didn't want to think about a scenario where Zach wouldn't be here next year. "It's too early to plan."

"It's never too early, or too late, to go after what you want."

"Very poetic," I teased with a smirk.

"I'm serious, Poppy."

I licked my suddenly dry lips. "You'll be hundreds of miles away next year. Long distance never works."

"Quit inventing problems."

God, it was like he could read my mind. A heavy sigh escaped my lips at this almost impossible scenario.

"There isn't a single problem that can't be solved with great sex," he added, eyes still trained on mine.

He spoke the words with such conviction, like he

knew them to be true. And for a second I wondered if he was right. My body grew warm under his appraisal and I shifted in my seat to alleviate the sudden ache between my legs. As I lifted my wineglass to my lips, our server appeared with our meals.

Grateful for the distraction of our food, I tasted a bite of pasta while Zach cut a piece of his chicken marsala and popped it into his mouth. Maybe if I could just pretend like that part of the conversation never happened, we could move on.

"This place is really good," I said, forcing myself to hold back from saying all the things I couldn't to Zach— like the fact that I was attracted to him too, unbelievably, and that I'd never had *great* sex in my entire life. Jason's idea of foreplay was to remove his glasses. None of that would be productive to my education, to my writing, or to chasing my dreams and showing Connor that life was what you made it. I couldn't trade it all for a few mind-blowing orgasms. I wouldn't.

And most of all, I wanted to tell him about Connor—about becoming a mom before I graduated high school, that my responsibility toward my son colored every decision I made.

Plus, Zach was leaving. He had plans to move to New York next year. Even if anything could come of this, we were doomed before we could even begin.

He chewed his food slowly, still studying me. "Their whole family moved here from Italy. Everything is homemade daily. And I probably eat here way too often, but I love this place."

While we ate, we kept to safe topics—which of Ariel's poems were our favorites, places he'd traveled, places we wanted to travel, and the merits of traditional versus self-publishing.

After sharing a tiramisu, I thought the night couldn't be any more perfect. Great poetry, great food, great conversation, and a man who was so nice to look at—even if I'd never let myself touch.

As we stepped into the night air, Zach gestured around the corner. "My place is actually right here, if you want another glass of wine."

I couldn't help but laugh. "Oh, it just happens to be around the corner? I'm sure that's entirely a coincidence."

He put up his hands, but he was laughing. "Me? Plan something like that?"

I bit my lip. It had been a fun night, and the idea of going home alone wasn't very appealing at that moment. I hated the nights Connor stayed with my parents. Plus, I was totally curious to see where Zach lived.

"Alright, I'll come in. But just one drink."

His house was a cute, old craftsman with wood floors and high ceilings.

"This is nice," I said, impressed as he led me inside.

"You sound surprised," he said, hanging up his coat in a hall closet.

"No offense, but I pictured you having a total bachelor pad." I spun around, taking in the detailed molding. I followed him into the kitchen, which had brand new granite countertops. "This is amazing. I love the picture frame molding on the walls in the entryway."

He nodded. "I just put that in, actually. I'm still working on some things, but it's coming along."

I watched Zach as he grabbed a bottle of wine and started twisting it open. He really was full of surprises. He knew my favorite writer, picked out amazing restaurants, *and* he knew how to fix up a house? *I wonder what else he's got in his toolbox, a screwdriver or hammer that I could use*, I thought before mentally slapping myself. Alone with Zach at his house after a romantic evening wasn't the right time to start getting horny. I needed to stay strong.

As we settled into the couch with our wine, I slipped my shoes off.

"This was really fun, seriously, thanks for inviting me." I pulled my hair out from the tight bun I'd put it in earlier and shook it out. "I probably needed to let loose a little bit."

Zach watched my hair fall from its updo, his breath hitching as he observed me. My brain not-so-helpfully supplied all the ways Zach could help me let loose— preferably with his hands on my skin.

I tried to be casual, but his nearness had made my body heat up a few degrees.

"I'm glad you said yes." Zach took a sip of his own wine and set his glass down on the table. "Did you ever figure out who was writing you those poems?"

I shook my head. "You?"

Zach drew a shallow inhale, and met my gaze. "Whoever he is, he seems like he really wants a shot with you."

It wasn't exactly an answer, but I didn't want to talk about that just now anyway. I was here alone with Zach and determined to enjoy my rare evening out.

"Listen, Poppy. I talk a big game. I know this about myself. But I need you to promise me one thing."

I rolled my eyes.

"This is serious, Poppy. Will you promise?"

"What am I promising?" This man had a way of getting me to say things, to feel things, to admit things that I might not have otherwise. I wasn't sure if it was because he was older and wiser and that much more cunning at these types of discussions, or if it was just because being near him seemed to physically lower my inhibitions. He was like a walking shot of tequila.

"I need you to promise me that if anything physical happens between us—that it will be very consensual, and very sex-positive. I need you to understand that I will worship you and make you come So. Many. Fucking. Times."

He enunciated those words so clearly and slowly, I

felt them with every beat of my heart, every pulse of heat between my legs.

Oblivious to my hammering heart, Zach continued. "But I also need you to know that if I do or say anything you don't like, all you have to do is say so and everything will stop. Just the word no, Poppy. Use it and I promise to leave you alone."

"Leave me alone as in stop mentoring me, stop helping me in the program?"

His face was serious and he shook his head without even considering it. "I will never stop mentoring you, as long as you want it. Giving in to our attraction—or not—will never be a condition for my help. I want you to succeed, and it has nothing to do with how much I want you in my bed. Do you understand that?"

I felt myself nodding my head.

I knew what he was saying. Despite how aggressively Zach put his feelings on the subject of us out there—I knew he'd never betray my wishes.

"Okay," I murmured.

He considered me for a long moment, neither of us blinking.

"Why did you approach me that night at the party, Poppy. Did you find me attractive?"

Was he fucking serious?

Of course I find him attractive. Actually, attractive was too weak a word. I found him mesmerizing. Addictive. Enchanting. Impossible.

"I'm not saying I do, but if I wanted something to happen ..." I swallowed a wave of nerves and took a shallow breath as Zach's mouth curved into a grin.

"*Something* as in finding out how many times in a row I can make you come using my mouth, my hands, and my ..."

I held up one hand. "Yes. That. How would it work, isn't it, like, forbidden?"

God, why did the word forbidden make me feel even hotter?

Zach's gaze wandered to the distance for a moment, like he was lost in thought. "The university's rules on this aren't written in the employee handbook."

Oh my God, had he actually checked? Why did that thought make my cheeks heat?

"Student / professor relationships are the only thing addressed," he added, his tone serious.

"And?"

"And if I was a professor who was pursing you this way—I'd lose my job."

"Oh."

"Yes."

"But you're not a professor."

"I'm not. But still ...The possibility is there, which makes this dangerous."

"Then why are we discussing this Zach? We both know nothing can happen between us." Except I felt more confused now than ever.

"Even if you wanted it to?"

God, what did I want? His dark emerald gaze returned to mine, burning so bright and hot that I felt it deep inside me. "I rarely seem to get what I want these days."

"We could change that."

I took another sip of my wine and looked over at

him. He was so damned attractive. So masculine and intense. What if we just stopped fighting this attraction? What if I just decided to loosen up a bit, push the boundaries, say fuck the rules … I wasn't sure if it was the wine, or this man, but suddenly the idea of testing the waters appealed to me more and more.

I set my wine down and moved closer to Zach on the couch. I looked into his eyes, which had suddenly turned serious. *God, how did he do that?* This man had the power to turn my insides molten with just one sizzling look.

I'd cataloged *repeatedly* all the reasons why this couldn't happen. But right now? None of them seemed to matter. I wanted his lips on mine.

Knowing I had to be the one to show him what I wanted, I summoned my courage, and leaned in closer. Heat spread down my body as Zach's dark lust-filled eyes cataloged my movements.

Reaching toward him, I touched my fingertips to the stubble on his jaw. His eyes slid closed as my fingers explored. He didn't move—didn't speak—didn't so much as breathe—as I got closer. It was almost like he wasn't sure I was actually going to go through with this. Like if he moved, the spell would be broken.

As I scooted even closer to him on the couch, his eyes reopened.

"Zach," I murmured.

His eyes surveyed mine like he was searching for the answer to a question, and once he was sure he could touch me, Zach reached out a hand and cupped my cheek, pulling me in closer until our lips were almost touching. I closed my eyes and let out a little moan as he gripped my hair into a fist.

His mouth closed over mine. It wasn't the slow, cautious kiss of our first time. It was hungry and passionate, like he'd thought of nothing else every day since our first kiss. He sucked on my tongue, tangled my hair in his fist and made the most fantastic groaning sound.

Without breaking our kiss, I swung my leg over his so that I was straddling him. While his tongue slid sensually with mine, his hands slid down my back, leaving my skin tingling everywhere he'd touched.

Our new position made it impossible to ignore his denim-clad erection, which was now nudging restlessly between my legs. "Shit," I moaned.

Cupping my ass in his palms, Zach let out a ragged groan. "You are so fucking perfect." His mouth teased the side of my neck, my jaw, leaving sweet little sucking kisses.

"We shouldn't," I breathed.

"I know. But this feels too good, too right." He tugged me closer to his erection—so it nudged at my center—and I made a helpless cry of pleasure. "You feel it too. I know you do," he grunted. "Tell me, Poppy."

He was right, so right. My heart pounded in my throat, and as his tongue slid into my mouth I instinctively put my hands on his chest and gripped his shirt, pulling myself closer against him so our bodies were pressed even tighter together. My mind was totally blank, everything was taken over by how much I craved his touch. He slipped a hand under my shirt, and I inhaled sharply as his hand touched my bare skin. My breasts ached as my nipples hardened, anticipating his touch. Zach's hand slid up to cup my breast while his tongue continued moving expertly against mine.

I was so wet, so incredibly turned on, that I began

rocking against him, imagining how good it would feel to repeat this entire scenario without clothes—to ride him, and feel him inside me. Because Zach might be my academic adviser and this scenario was definitely taboo, but holy hell, he had a huge cock. Unable to stop myself, I pushed my hips faster, rocking harder against him.

"So fucking sexy. Can you come like this?"

For a moment, I thought I might—come just from rubbing up against him, and his obscene erection pulsing beneath me.

I let out a low moan of pleasure, and shook my head. Zach shifted, lifting me in his arms, and placed me flat on my back on his couch.

I mourned the loss of him, but then smiled when I saw he had something much better in mind. Lowering himself on top of me, I let out a contented sigh as Zach's body weight moved over mine. All that hard muscle hovering over me—I felt safe, cherished.

"You have no idea how badly I want you," he said, shifting his hips forward experimentally so I could feel the hard ridge of him.

I bit back a giggle. "I have some idea."

Parting my thighs, I invited him closer, and Zach lowered his mouth to mine once again, rocking in tiny thrusts into me as we continued kissing.

"I want to make you come, Poppy."

The way his body moved, the powerful muscles in his back, the attention he paid to the smallest details—like tasting the spot where my pulse flickered in my neck—all of these things told me he'd be an amazing lover.

And dear God, how I longed to find out. To discover all the secret ways he could bring my body pleasure.

"Need to touch you," he groaned a sound that sounded a lot like frustration. "Tell me it's okay, tell me you want this too."

I nodded, eyes on his, and watched as his large hands moved down to the button on my jeans. Watching in stunned fascination as he tugged my jeans down to my knees, pulling my panties down with them. Zach kneeled on the couch between my legs, his eyes caressing me everywhere.

"Fuck, you are so sexy." He stroked me carefully with his thumb, pressing against my swollen clit.

I let out a shuddering moan.

"I need to make that sexy little pussy come."

I'd barely let out a noise of approval when Zach lowered his lips to the warm, swollen flesh between my legs and gave me a slow kiss that stole all the oxygen from my lungs.

Soon, Zach was eating me like I was his last meal, his hot mouth all over me, licking and sucking like his life depended on it, while his stubble burned my thighs.

"Can I fuck you with my fingers, Poppy?" he asked, voice whisper-soft and rough.

"Y-yes," I managed on a broken sob.

Two thick fingers speared into me and my mouth dropped open in a silent moan as I watched his muscled forearm with its sexy ink flex as he drove into me.

Dear God …

"So sweet and tempting." He gave me another slow lick. "My flesh rises at your name." Another wet kiss. "You drive me mad with want," he whispered dirty words to me each time he came up for air.

While his fingers slid in and out, my body made wet,

sucking sounds. The pleasure was nearly overwhelming, and as desperate as I was to have him inside me—it was the way the man quoted freaking Shakespeare while we were being intimate that was my undoing.

His mouth lowered to my clit once again while his fingers continued coaxing and soon, the orgasm that had been building came barreling down on me. I gripped his head, pushing my fingers into his hair, holding his mouth to my core.

Zach was fused tight, his tongue doing the most delicious dance over my swollen flesh until I cried out and jerked against him, grinding out every last ounce of pleasure. It had been so long, and I'd wanted him from the first moment I spotted him—I was powerless.

I came in a powerful rush—clenching down on his fingers—gasping out his name. Zach's eyes opened and lifted to mine, while his tongue continued slowly coaxing each aftershock from my body.

He rose to his knees, still watching me. His tented jeans and flashing eyes, his beautifully powerful shoulders all bunched with tension... He was the sexiest, most masculine thing I'd ever seen. His hand remained on my naked hip, his thumb tracing small circles over my skin.

Dear God…

I wanted to pounce on him, wanted to ride him like a bull at the rodeo, wanted to feel those powerful muscles under my fingers, but then my brain snapped back on, plunging me into the unwelcome reality of our situation.

"Wait," I breathed.

His hand slid from my skin, and he watched me, lips parted, both of us breathing hard. "Too fast?"

"Too … everything. I can't."

He rose from the couch and I didn't miss the discreet way he adjusted the enormous erection in his pants. A pang of momentary regret pulsed through me again.

"Poppy." His voice was ragged, and he was still breathing hard.

I forced myself to meet his eyes. He looked as taken aback as I was.

"I'm sorry, I'm just …" It's not that I didn't want to, but I knew I couldn't get involved with him. It wouldn't be smart. And I always played it safe, always did what was right.

"Poppy," he said again, composing himself. "If you really don't want this, I'll stop. Everything will stop. But you have to honestly tell me you don't want me."

I was still catching my breath and I felt torn in two different directions. He was watching me intently, waiting for my decision. I stood up and grabbed my shoes. "I don't want this."

It was a bold-faced lie, and terrified that Zach would see straight through me, I left his house as quickly as I could, without looking back. I felt tears spring into my eyes and roughly wiped them away. What was wrong with me? Of course, I wanted him, but I was here to succeed in school, not to fuck my adviser. What would Connor think if I got kicked out of school for sleeping with a faculty member? What would my parents say? They'd say they'd been right all along, that being a writer wasn't practical, that it was too difficult, and I didn't want it bad enough. That I should just get an average job like them and accept a mediocre life. Well, I wanted something more. It was what I'd been trying to prove ever since I moved out of their house and decided to pursue my dream, even though it wasn't easy and there were so many uncertainties. And what would Connor think if I didn't finish this degree?

Pursue your dreams until a cute guy comes along, then throw it all away? No. No way. No matter how much I wanted Zach, I'd worked too hard to be a good role model and prove I could achieve anything I set my mind to.

Chapter Thirteen

Zach

The fucking thermostat was broken again. After getting my laptop set up and connected to the projector at the front of the classroom, I pulled my sweater off and shoved it in my bag. Being dressed in just a t-shirt and jeans wasn't the most professional, but the university didn't have a strict dress code for the staff, and I really didn't feel like leading this presentation while sweating my balls off.

I walked across the room and read the digital thermostat. It was stuck on seventy-eight degrees, just as I suspected. I'd call building maintenance later, but right now, there was no time. The first students were filing in and taking seats around the room. I couldn't help but notice Poppy wasn't among them. For a moment, I wondered if maybe she wouldn't show up at all, then decided that wasn't Poppy. No matter how confusing things were between us, Poppy was nothing if not professional. She would be here.

But as more students filtered in, and the small auditorium was nearly full, I couldn't help but wonder if she was going to purposefully arrive late, just so she didn't have to chance finding me alone in the classroom. Because really, what was there to say to each other? We'd gone out on an amazing date, gone back to my place and shared an amazing kiss. God, it was just a kiss. But when had kissing been like that? So raw and wild and passionate? I thought about the way she'd climbed into my lap, rocking her pussy up against my cock. And then things had escalated quickly from there, until I'd pulled down her jeans and panties to bury my face between her thighs. And when Poppy had come all over my mouth?

Christ.

I had to take a deep breath, and refocus myself so I didn't become aroused in front of a classroom full of students. Poppy had been so perfect—so soft and responsive in my arms, making the most adorably sexy cries of pleasure as I kissed her and touched her. But then something changed in her and everything had stopped.

I knew on paper we didn't make sense. I got that. But I was willing to say fuck it and at least try—to see where things went. But apparently, she wasn't.

I knew when I saw her, I'd have to pretend that nothing had happened between us. I'd have to be professional and civil, not cold or unfeeling in any way that might make her think I was bothered by what she'd said or done when she left me high and dry on Saturday night. Because truly I wasn't upset about that. Sex should be positive and safe, and comfortable and if Poppy wasn't ready for that, I would wait. What bothered me the most was that she was shutting down any remote possibility of their being an *us*.

But I also knew we couldn't continue on the way we'd been. I couldn't offer her secret smiles or tease her in front of her fellow students. I couldn't even do that in private anymore. I needed to be the adult here and respect her wishes. And her wish—at least, the one she was willing to say out loud—was to never see me in a romantic capacity again.

I took my spot at the front of the classroom, and when I looked up—there she was. With her laptop bag slung over her shoulder, and dressed in an oversized sweater and leggings, Poppy looked irresistible.

I was supposed to be presenting on the internships, fellowships, and grants available for these student writers. Instead my brain was occupied with thoughts of one student in particular—the infuriatingly perfect girl who didn't even trust herself to meet my gaze.

I couldn't help the frown that tugged on my mouth while I watched her find an open seat. She pulled out a notebook and pen, readying herself for the presentation, and never made eye contact. That fact alone stung more than everything else.

Yet, after everything we shared, it was as though Poppy was ready to wipe me from her memory. As badly as I wanted things to be different, I was starting to realize that perhaps it was time to move on.

But then her gaze fell on me, and I was all too aware of the bright blush that painted her cheeks. I was careful to sweep past her, focusing instead on a girl with bushy eyebrows a few rows behind her.

"Hello everyone. Some of you already know me as your advisor, but my name is Zach Austin, and we're here today to talk about the most important thing in the world."

I glanced around the room again, studying one student's set of SpongeBob pajama pants before pointing to the boy they belonged to.

"What's your name?"

"Tad."

"Ok, Tad," I said. "How is your semester going?"

"Busy." The boy shrugged.

"Busy." I nodded. "Right. I'm sure that's the case for all of you. I'm not an idiot. I know most of you work full-time, some of you have families, and on top of that you're going to three-hour-long classes to advance your career." I clapped. "That's a lot for anyone. Which is why I have some bad news for you. It only gets worse from here."

Silence greeted my words and I sat back on the desk behind me, bracing myself against the wooden top. Pointing to the girl behind Poppy, I said, "Have you thought about your thesis at all?"

The woman blinked. "I mean, I wrote about it in my declaration of intent when I applied."

"But since then. What have you done with it?"

"Well..." She looked around. "It's been busy."

"Ah. And here's where we come to the important part. See, I don't hold this little graduate pow-wow because I like seeing all your smiling faces. I do it because I need you to understand something—It. Only. Gets. Worse. From. Here. Just like most schooling, graduate school is going to get harder over time so that little idea you had for a thesis when you were applying to study here? You need to flesh it out. You need to explore it. You need to work on it whenever you have a free moment because free moments are going to become very hard to come by. And two years isn't that long."

A few of the students looked at each other and Poppy glanced down at her open notebook, her cheeks still a bright, pretty pink.

Don't.

"This week, I encourage all of you to drill down into your thesis projects and really figure out what you need to do to succeed and get on the right schedule. Talk to your advisors. Learn to trust them. They have your best interest at heart, truly."

Poppy scribbled something in her notebook, but I continued to ignore her, looking at another girl with auburn hair and splotchy red spots on her face. She raised her hand and I pointed to her.

"Yes?"

"Can you go over the finer points of the thesis?"

I turned to the board, doing as she asked while bullet pointing the more fundamental parts of the project.

When I turned around, though, Poppy's hand was in the air.

My heart dropped into my gut, but I pointed to her all the same. "Yes?"

"Does the English Symposium on campus count toward our final graded presentation?"

"No," I said simply, then swept to the other side of the room. "Now, keep in mind that the department offers lots of scholarships and grants toward furthering your learning. I implore you to look into them and discuss your options with your advisor. For any other questions, you can also look to your adviser for help. They are your lifeline here on campus. Trust them."

I raised my eyebrows.

"Any other questions?"

When the room was silent again, I clapped my hands together. "Great, now get out there and seize the day. Good luck on your midterms. Good luck on those thesis projects."

I stalked back toward my desk and grabbed my briefcase quickly, careful not to look behind me at the meandering, shuffling students as I climbed the stairs again and bolted for my office. If I did, I was sure I would find Poppy's gaze trailing after me, all her unspoken questions hanging in the air between us.

But today was not going to be about Poppy. Not again. Today was the first day of the rest of my life and I was determined to move on, take my own advice, and dive into my work with all the gusto it required to finally get my manuscript finished.

A knock sounded on my door and I glanced up to find Poppy in the open doorframe, her backpack slung lazily over one shoulder.

Today her hair was pulled into a tight ponytail and her oversized sweater had slid off of one shoulder, exposing the delicate skin.

"Yes?" I said. "How can I help you?"

She bit her bottom lip then stepped into my office and shut the door behind her. "I was hoping you had a few minutes to talk to me."

"What about?" I asked, trying again to feign nonchalance as my pulse pounded in my ears.

I couldn't escape the memories of grinding her pussy into my face—the scent of her all warm and feminine and sweet.

She swallowed hard and then dropped into the seat opposite my desk. "I think I might be better off with a new advisor."

"I'm sorry?" I asked, raising my eyebrows and pretending that wasn't like a sucker punch straight to the windpipe.

She glanced at the corner of the room, then forced herself to meet my gaze. "I think I ought to get a new advisor. You just talked so much in the meeting about how there needs to be a good partnership between advisor and advisee and how your advisor is your lifeline and—"

"And you don't think I can be that for you," I prompted, my voice chilly.

She shook her head. "It's not that. You're a great adviser and you've really improved my work, but I feel like if we continue on this way—"

"You can't trust me to be professional?" I tried again.

"Look, Zach."

"Poppy, " I said, folding my hands on the desk in front of me. "You don't have anything to worry about. The most important thing here is your work. You can trust me to respect your boundaries and remain professional. But, if you feel there's another member of the faculty who would suit your needs better, you are certainly welcome to change your advisor."

"You've been helpful. I just feel...well, you barely looked at me in there." She gestured toward the hall. "I…didn't like it. Or the way it made me feel."

"I think you might be reading into things. Give it time, and everything will go back to normal."

She nodded. "Yeah, okay, maybe. I know I sound fickle and I just want…"

"Look, this is what you said you wanted, Poppy. I'm trying but you've got to give me a little leeway to find my feet, okay?"

"Yeah. Yeah, I understand."

"Great. Now is there anything else you need help with?"

"No, I think I'm okay."

It was clear she wasn't. Neither of us was, but what else was there to say?

"Excellent." A moment of tension weighed on the space between us and then she straightened her backpack on her shoulder and made her way back to the door.

"Okay, well, thanks for talking it out with me."

"Any time. What are advisors for?"

She disappeared through the door, thankfully shutting it again behind her so I could lay my head on my desk and think of all the ways I could have handled myself better. I didn't know how it would be normal to ever be around her again, not when my libido was screaming at me even now to chase after her, but I knew I needed to move on...

Since my brain was so spun up over thoughts of Poppy, I decided a good old-fashioned dose of testosterone might do me some good. It was either that, or lose my fucking marbles over a case of blue balls.

One of my best friends from my college, Brandon, was always hassling me about coming out with the guys in his bowling league, and I'd always adamantly refused. But earlier this week, I'd texted him to find out if the offer still stood. Of course, he'd replied, which is how I found myself pulling into a rundown tavern at nine o'clock on a work night. Brandon said his league came here after their games for cheap beer and hot wings.

It was just the sort of masculine activity to keep my head on straight.

"Hey! There he is." Brandon rose to his feet when he spotted me across the bar, and waved me over to their table near the bar. "Can't believe you actually fucking came," he said, motioning to the empty chair beside him. "Guys, this is Zach."

"Hey." I gave a non-committal half-wave. "You guys

win tonight?"

There were grumbles and some curse words traded among the half-dozen or so men and that, paired with the six pitchers of beer on the table, gave me all the answer I needed. "Better luck next time."

Brandon shrugged. "Ignore them. The league we competed against tonight is notoriously shitty, so we thought we had this one in the bag. Played too fast and loose. We'll be golden next week."

I nodded, watched the waitress approach. "Another pint glass, or would you like to order something different?"

"Yeah, bring him a glass," Brandon said.

"And a round of shots for the table. Something strong. Patrón?" I asked, handing her my credit card.

She nodded. "Right away."

"Thanks, buddy. You didn't have to do that," Brandon said.

I settled in, pouring myself a glass of beer, and listening while my friend filled me in on the latest. Brandon was recently married to his college sweetheart, and they were talking about trying for a baby soon.

"Holy shit, man. That's huge. Congrats." I gave him a thump on the back.

He shot me a smirk. "So, what gives, man? I've invited you out with us a dozen times. Why now? Why tonight?"

I'd been hoping to avoid this question. And thought I'd be able to. Brandon's fun, but he isn't the most perceptive person in the world.

I took another swig of my beer, stalling. "You picked up on that, huh?"

He shot me a pointed stare. "Doesn't take a rocket scientist to figure out something's up, dude."

I shrugged. "I suppose not."

Our shots were delivered, and the guys lifted their glasses, toasting to next week, and then Brandon was looking at me again from over the rim of his beer glass. "You writing anything lately?" he asked.

"Been working on something, yeah."

He shook his head. "I don't get how you do that."

"What? Write a book?"

He nodded.

I chuckled. "It's not as hard as it seems."

He shrugged. "The first few pages, maybe, even a chapter, sure. But an entire book? It's beyond me, man."

I considered his sentiment. It was funny, because when I first began writing I used to feel the same way. I remembered the pain of having to write my first twenty-page paper in high school.

"You just don't stop," I said, like that cleared everything up.

Brandon shook his head. "If you say so. Hey, thanks again for looking out for Josh at that party."

"Of course."

My brain helpfully supplied that it was that party—that chance encounter where I'd first met Poppy.

"So, anyone special in your life?" Brandon asked. "I've gotta tell you, married life is pretty fucking awesome, bro."

He grinned at me, and the desire to punch him square in the jaw flared up out of nowhere. I took a long drink of my beer instead.

"Not a fucking soul," I said.

He grinned at me. "Might be able to help you there…"

Chapter Fourteen

Poppy

"Boo!"

I nearly screamed, jumping back on the sidewalk, before realizing the sound had come from an automated decoration in my neighbor's Halloween display. *Jesus, I must really be on edge.*

I usually didn't scare at the sight of a cheap plastic ghost, but ever since the night I'd gone home with Zach I'd been feeling jumpy and anxious. *The night you rejected Zach*, I reminded myself. I had avoided being alone with him after that night, which proved to be a bigger feat than I'd expected. I'd had to pull some serious ninja moves around campus to dodge him. I knew I was being childish, but I'd been feeling a mixture of embarrassment and regret; we'd had a great time and then I totally freaked out, running out of there like a crazy person.

Maybe a grand gesture would fix things? I thought about what Zach would do if I dressed up as a slutty nurse and showed up at his door. Last week I would have confidently said he'd pull me inside, rip off my costume and do all the things I'd been fantasizing about him doing to me, but now I wouldn't be surprised if he shut the door in my face. He'd put himself out there, and I'd rejected him, it was as simple as that. I just wasn't brave enough to start something—and not just because he was my adviser—I wasn't brave enough to begin another relationship period. And Zach was leaving anyways. Just like men always left. Especially once they discovered how much of my time was devoted to Connor.

As I walked in the front door my thoughts were interrupted by Kody tossing a plastic bag in my direction. He and Jodee had been watching Connor while I ran a couple of errands. I caught it, giving him a questioning look. "What is this?" I asked.

"It's your costume."

Kody was wearing a plaid sweater vest and slacks. Jodee walked into the living room from the kitchen wearing a checkered dress and an apron.

"Why are you guys dressed like that?" I opened the plastic bag and pulled out a pale pink onesie and a plastic baby rattle.

"What the…" I started.

"You're a baby." Kody grinned.

"And we're your parents," Jodee chimed in.

Kody had texted me last week that he had an idea for our costumes and I'd assumed I could trust him to pick something out. I was clearly wrong.

"Why do I have to be the baby?" I asked. "I *have* a baby."

"Exactly, you are the most qualified to *be* a baby since you *raised* a baby," Kody threw back at me.

As if on cue, Connor looked up from the toy cars he was playing with on the floor, making tiny buzzing sounds with his mouth to imitate the engine.

"Connor, don't you think your mom will look cute as a baby for Halloween?" Kody asked. Connor's face screwed up like he was trying to imagine it before he burst out laughing. He jumped up, running around the house shouting, "Mom's a baby, Mom's a baby."

"He's never going to stop saying that now," I told Kody, but I couldn't help but laugh about how ridiculous it all was.

"Trust me this is a great costume," Kody said,

standing up and adjusting his fake glasses in the mirror. "We should hurry or we're going to be late for the contest."

* * *

After dropping Connor off at my parents' house for the night we headed to the Hog's Head, a bar popular for their annual Halloween party. I'd hesitated at first, not wanting to be away from Connor all night, but my parents had practically forced me out the door. I never expected to be at a point where my sixty-year-old parents were telling me to get a life, and I figured I should take it as a sign that I needed to get out more. Plus, Halloween technically wasn't until Sunday night, so I wouldn't miss trick or treating with Connor.

Hog's Head was packed with students and locals, all eager to win the costume contest. The bar had been decorated with cobwebs and fake spiders and they were serving a specialty Halloween drink that was called "monster's blood." Kody surveyed the room, assessing everyone's chances of winning the contest.

"Okay, I think our biggest challenger is them," he said, pointing to a group of friends dressed as Kiss.

"Damn, they look really convincing," Jodee said, standing on her tiptoes to get a better look.

"I still think we can win," Kody said confidently.

We pushed our way through the crowd, trying to get to the bar. I had to duck to dodge someone's plastic scythe from poking me in the eye, and when I stood back up and caught sight of the bar my heart stopped.

Zach.

He was standing at the bar talking to someone, but I couldn't see who through the crowd. Of course, he hadn't dressed up and he looked effortlessly sexy as always in black jeans and a gray t-shirt. I thought about walking out right then. Away from him, away from this crazy attraction that made me feel dizzy. But I didn't. I snuck another look at him instead.

Even now, the sight of him sent my heart fluttering and brought me back to that kiss at his house. I'd had quick flashes of it ever since that night, which seemed to be totally out of my control. Just the thought of it was enough to get my heart pounding in my chest. I'd been so turned on that that night, walking away had been almost impossible. But it had been the right thing. Right?

That's what I kept telling myself. But the memory of Zach's lips on my neck, his hands anchoring my waist to his lap, where I writhed and rocked until I almost came—fully clothed—on top of him. And then after when he'd quoted Shakespeare and asked if he could fuck me with his fingers.

Shit. I shook my head.

Maybe I should say something, go and clear the air. How could he stay upset with me when I was wearing a baby costume?

I had started to fight my way over to him when the crowd parted for a second and I saw who it was he was talking to.

Oh, hell no.

He was with a woman. She was tall, and blonde and dressed in a black leotard that said Barbie, pink tights, black knee-high socks and pink accessories. I rolled my eyes. *Seriously?*

I was frozen to the spot, until Zach's date whispered something in his ear and headed toward the ladies' room. My stomach knotted and I had to remind myself to breathe. The noise of the crowd had gone silent, everything fading away into the background. Without thinking, I pushed my way through the crowd and walked right up to him. Even in my state I couldn't help but compare this moment to the night we met, me walking up to Zach in the middle of a crowded room, except this time I was pissed off.

"So, you're fucking Barbie now?"

Zach turned to me, startled, and looked me up and down, taking in my baby costume. He smirked.

"Her name's Stacey. And no, I haven't fucked her." He paused, his green eyes drilling into mine, making my heartbeat speed up a few paces. "I haven't even kissed her, actually."

I crossed my arms. "So, what, you're on a date?"

He sighed, exasperated. "You told me to move on, that we couldn't be together. What was I supposed to do? Wait for you? You were very clear, Poppy. It doesn't matter how much I want you, if you don't want me back …"

Tears sprung into my eyes and I swallowed hard to keep them from falling. I took a deep breath, releasing whatever adrenaline had caused me to confront Zach in the first place.

"You're right." My voice cracked and I wasn't quite able to meet his eyes. "I'm sorry."

His brows knitted in frustration and Zach shook his head. "I am too."

I turned and pushed my way through the crowd, not waiting to hear if Zach had anything else to say. What else was there to say? It was selfish of me to reject him and then be mad that he was trying to move on. I just hadn't expected him to move on so quickly. Who was I kidding, Jason moved on in less time than it took me to down a sushi roll, so why was I expecting anything different from Zach.

I found Kody and Jodee at the other end of the bar. Without saying anything to them, I signaled the bartender.

"Three tequila shots," I shouted over the noise. Kody and Jodee gave each other a look.

"What's up? You look like you're about to cry," Jodee said, concern in her voice.

I pointed in the direction of Zach and Stacey, who had returned from the bathroom and was batting her eyelashes at Zach and giving him pouty looks. Kody and Jodee both gasped.

"Who is that? Is he on a date?"

I nodded miserably.

"But he's right, I'm the one who said I didn't want anything to happen," I said, voice still quavering.

Jodee hugged me. "I'm sorry, Poppy."

"She's not even cute," Kody said, leaning over to get a better view.

I forced a smile. "Thanks, guys, but it's okay, let's just have fun tonight." I didn't want to be a downer and ruin the night, especially after seeing how excited Kody was about the costume contest. I also didn't want Zach to see my friends staring him and his date down from across the bar.

They were still giving me concerned looks, so I held up my tequila shot.

Paraphrasing F. Scott Fitzgerald, I toasted to each of my friends, "Too much of anything is bad, but too much tequila is just right. Drink up, my friends."

They didn't look convinced, but they went along with

my toast. After downing the shots, I ordered a cup of 'monster's blood', which sounded gross but was actually fruit punch and vodka. I was feeling slightly less miserable once the alcohol kicked in, but I still couldn't stop myself from sneaking glances at Zach and Stacey, who were laughing and flirting at the bar. Of course she was having a good time. Zach was sweet, funny, sexy, a total catch. A total catch that I'd rejected. *Seriously, stop moping*, I told myself.

Everything that had happened had been my choice, and I needed to accept it. There was no way I could keep up with school and raising Connor if I lost myself in Zach. Not to mention the complications with him being my adviser. It was just that being around Zach—and the copious amounts of alcohol I was consuming tonight— made it incredibly difficult to remember what about this situation was so wrong. I sighed and turned to find my friends when I walked straight into Chad, a tall, blond poet in my workshop, dressed as the Joker from Batman.

"Hey, Poppy," he said, looking me up and down. "You're a…"

"A baby," I said, shrugging. I'd accepted that my outfit made me the least sexy person at the bar and was glad I could at least be comfortable.

He laughed. "I get it, it's cute. So how are you liking the program so far?"

"Everything is going great," I lied.

We continued to talk about school and discuss the latest poems we'd been writing.

"Can I buy you a drink?" he asked at a break in the conversation.

I hesitated. Chad and I were friendly, but I'd always gotten the feeling he had a crush on me, and I didn't want to lead him on. I glanced over at Zach, who was cracking up about something Stacey had just said.

Fuck it.

"Sure," I said, turning back to Chad with a smile. "That sounds great."

After taking yet another tequila shot with Chad, we continued to talk about school. I tried to focus on the conversation but couldn't stop my mind from wandering. I couldn't see Zach anymore and wondered what he and bitchy Barbie were up to. After a few more minutes of trying and failing to pay attention to Chad, I told him I needed to find my friends. I just wasn't interested in him, and it was becoming painfully obvious.

"Can we go?" I asked after I'd found Kody and Jodee by the DJ. I stumbled a bit as I walked up to them.

"Whoa, how much have you drunk?" Jodee asked.

"I'm fine," I said, waving her off. "But seriously, can we leave?"

"Five more minutes, please," Kody begged. "They're about to announce the winners of the group contest and I'm pretty sure we have a shot."

I sighed, resigning myself to a night of torture, when a man dressed as Frankenstein walked onstage.

"Alright, folks, it's time to select the winners of the contest. All groups to the stage first."

Kody grabbed my arm and towed me up the steps to the stage.

Jodee followed and the three of us stood in the center of the stage, flanked by a group of guys dressed as a hockey team, and a group of girls dressed up as Playboy bunnies.

As much as it pained me, my eyes found Zach. He

had stopped talking to Barbie and stood there staring at me. I felt his gaze like it was licks of fire and I was ablaze.

After making a big show of opening the envelope, Frankenstein grinned and shouted out four names I didn't recognize. The Kiss group stepped forward, high fiving the crowd. As they accept their prize of movie passes and certificates for free pizza, I headed down off the stage and toward the exit, my friends trailing after me. It looked like the only thing I was going to win that night was a massive hangover.

Chapter Fifteen

Zach

Last night was brutal.

I'd only agreed to go out with Brandon's single co-worker Stacey in a moment of weakness. She'd recently moved here, and Brandon gave me some speech about the difficulties of being new in a small town. She was nice enough, but then we'd run into Poppy, dressed adorably in a baby costume, and I was certain Stacey knew in that instant that I wasn't as single as I claimed to be. Because despite not actually being with Poppy, she owned me. Whether I wanted her to or not. She had cast a spell over me that refused to let go.

God, and her displeasure at seeing me with another woman? It was palpable.

I wanted to drop to my knees and pledge my allegiance to her, and I would have if I thought it would do any good.

But today, all I felt was sad. I felt bad for Poppy. Clearly, she had been as miserable as I was last night. I was just better at hiding it, but her emotions were as clear as day. She wanted me just as badly as I wanted her. And I didn't just want her for a quick fuck, but as a person in my life, someone to spend time with laughing, writing, doing mundane things like grocery shopping.

If I couldn't be with her, I at least wanted to continue our tortuous dance as friends. Grabbing my phone, I texted her to see how she was doing this morning.

Hey champ. How are you feeling this morning?

By the time I was out of the shower and dressed, I saw that she'd replied.

So awful. Bring me Tylenol? I promise I'll bake you so many chocolate chip cookies. So many. Please.

I chuckled at her text, but then a wave of regret flashed through me and I felt even shittier because I realized that she was hungover because of me. If I hadn't brought a date and dangled another woman in her face, she wouldn't have over-indulged last night.

Of course I will. Just tell me your address.

A few seconds ticked by before she replied.

You really don't have to do that. My fault for drinking too much.

I shook my head. *I'm coming. Don't make me break into the student files to find out where you live.*

Her reply was immediate. *You wouldn't dare.*

Try me.

After Poppy caved and texted me her address, I grabbed my keys and wallet and was out the door and headed for the drug store a few minutes later.

It wasn't the promise of chocolate chip cookies that had me rushing to her, it was the opportunity to see Poppy with her guard down that had me all kinds of lit up. I wondered if seeing me with another woman had prompted Poppy's sudden new openness to seeing me. Or maybe she just needed pain killers that badly. I guess I'd find out.

When I arrived at her place, I parked on the street in front of the Victorian home that had been sectioned into two halves as most of the old homes on this street had been. They'd been sliced and diced into duplexes and apartments for students and as I walked up the front steps to the large home, I realized suddenly that Poppy had never mentioned a roommate, yet this place seemed too large for one.

My gaze lingered on the red boy's bike on the front porch as Poppy pulled open the front door.

"Hey," I started but Poppy thrust out a hand, motioning in a *gimme* gesture for the bag I was holding.

"Come in. And thank you. You're a lifesaver."

I followed her inside. She headed straight for the kitchen and pulled a bottle of water from the fridge before popping open the bottle of pain reliever and swallowing a couple of the pills.

"I have a massive headache, and I need to adult today. Thank you again."

My gaze wandered around her home, taking in the toys strewn on the living room floor, the framed photos of her with a little boy.

He looked so much like her. The wavy hair streaked with sunlight. The bright curious eyes. The delicate cheekbones and full mouth.

My heart hammered wildly. "Poppy?"

She drew a deep breath. "I have something I need to tell you."

I nodded, and followed as she led me over to the couch. We sat down together, and I sensed that everything I thought I knew, everything between us was about to change.

"I'm so sorry I didn't say anything before. That's Connor," she said simply, nodding toward the framed photo that hung on the wall.

"He's a handsome kid."

At that, she smiled and reached over and touched my hand.

"I'm sorry I kept him a secret. I never meant to. But I... I liked the way I felt around you—like a woman, and not just a mom. A regular student. I didn't mean to hide that side of myself, but I ..."

I shook my head, stopping her. "It's okay. There are things I never told you either." I thought about my last relationship, which had ended in a fucking mess, and my parents' own divorce that had colored every relationship I'd had since. "Let's just start over, okay?"

She drew another deep breath, and nodded. "Okay."

"How old is he?" I asked.

"Seven."

"So you had him … "

She nodded. "At the very end of high school."

Wow. All the respect and admiration I had for this woman was suddenly amplified ten-fold. All she must have been through, all the sacrifices she must have made.

"And you have full custody?"

She nodded again. "My high school boyfriend cut out before Connor was even born. I've been doing this on my own ever since."

"But you dated, you were recently single that night we met at the party."

She tucked her hair behind her ear and shifted. "I've dated, but not much. Most guys aren't okay with this side of my life, and even if they *say* they are, over time, it just becomes too much."

"I see." I couldn't help but wonder if my age, my maturity, the fact that I owned a home and had a stable career was a draw for her. Or maybe that was only wishful thinking. Still I wondered, did she crave that stability for her son? Had she only dated guys her age? I was almost thirty—and knew babies and kids were a part of my not-so-distant future. At least I'd hoped they were. But then I realized I'd acted so nonchalant about everything, telling her I was attracted to her, but never admitting I wanted something real. Poppy knew I wanted to fuck her and bring her pleasure, but did she know I wanted more too?

Footsteps on the other side of the door made us pause and look up.

"My mom's dropping Connor off," Poppy said rising to her feet.

I rose to stand beside her. "Is this a bad time, should I go?"

She shook her head.

And then there he was—the little boy who looked so much like the woman I'd fallen for. Dark hair and inquisitive, honey-colored eyes. When Connor spotted me in their living room, he stopped and frowned, staring at me as he remained rooted in place.

"Connor, this is my friend Zach. He works at the university," Poppy said.

Connor's frown eased. "Okay."

"Hello," I offered. "You ready for Halloween tomorrow?"

Connor frowned again. "I guess so."

"Come here, bud," Poppy encouraged. "Tell me about Grandma's. Did you have fun?"

He nodded as he approached, but he still looked bothered by something. I just prayed that it wasn't by my presence. I had enough strikes against me with his gorgeous mother.

Connor walked into his mom's embrace. She gave him a squeeze and placed a kiss on his forehead. "Tell me, lovey," she whispered.

My heart squeezed a little at the sight of him—this was all just so unexpected.

"My tooth is loose, and Sullivan said that his dad left him four dollars when he lost a tooth. It was under the pillow. I don't have a dad, how am I going to get the money for my tooth?"

Poppy sighed, and pushed a hand through her hair. Her mouth opened, then closed, and I placed my hand on her shoulder.

"I might be able to help you out there, buddy," I said, bending down so I was closer to Connor's height.

The little guy's eyes widened as he listened to me speak. The kid was freaking adorable. I loved the way his eyelashes resting on his cheeks reminded me of the way Poppy's did when she looked down, lost deep in thought. And I couldn't help but notice that Poppy watched in awe as I spoke to him, explaining that I grew up without my dad too.

"I know it sucks sometimes. But your mom works extra hard to make sure you have what you need. And I bet that she will be the one to leave the money under your pillow when you do lose your tooth."

He thought it over for half a second, his eyes narrowing. "But four dollars? That's a lot of money. The tooth fairy only left Eli a quarter."

I chuckled under my breath. The kid drove a hard bargain. He was a smart cookie, just like his pretty mother, apparently.

I pulled my wallet from my back pocket. "Tell you what." I grabbed four bills and placed them in his waiting palm. "Consider this a down payment."

Eyes still narrowed, Connor gazed down at the money and then back up at me. "But you're not my dad."

I shook my head. "No. I'm not. But I'm your mom's friend and I know what it's like to grow up without your dad in your life."

At this, his lips pressed together as if he was processing this information.

"And maybe when you're a grown-up man like me, you can pay it forward, help another little boy or girl someday."

Deciding he was happy with that answer, or just happy in general with those crisp bills in his hand, Connor gave me an enthusiastic nod. "Okay. I can do that."

He started to bound away when Poppy stopped him. "What do you say to Zach?"

"Thank you." He smiled at me, and then darted off, probably to stuff that money in his piggy bank before his mom said otherwise.

"You didn't have to do that," Poppy said, watching me cautiously.

"I know that. I wanted to. He reminds me of you. A

ton, actually."

At this, she finally smiled, and all was right with the world. It felt like I had finally won a piece of her over, this huge piece of her life that she hadn't been brave enough to share. Suddenly her hesitation at getting involved made perfect sense. It wasn't just herself she was thinking about. She had an entire future to protect, another little person she was responsible for. But we'd had enough heaviness for a moment. I decided to lighten the mood.

"So, about these chocolate chip cookies …"

Poppy gave a short laugh and rolled her eyes. "First, I need food."

My favorite diner had the best hangover food, and even better, the tables were covered in huge sheets of white paper and came with a big bowl of crayons.

"Get your stuff. I know just the place."

"But Connor…I can't leave him alone…" She sounded panicked, like I was just like the others, not realizing she came as a package deal. Oddly, it never even occurred to me that I should think of this little boy as an inconvenience. He was a huge part of Poppy's life I'd just been introduced to—and I know that Poppy even allowing me to cross that threshold and meet him was a huge milestone for her—and I was going to do everything in my power to make her understand that I was very okay with her and with Connor. Besides, she just added a MILF fantasy to my growing repertoire of spank bank material.

"I never expected you to leave him here, Poppy." And at that, I turned toward the kitchen.

I couldn't wait to see if Connor liked their chocolate chip pancakes as much as I did.

I waited in the kitchen while Poppy gathered Connor from his bedroom. Her home was neat and tidy, it felt homey and lived in. There were framed photographs on the walls, throw pillows and overstuffed ottomans, and gingham placemats on the dining table. I'd never envisioned Poppy as a mother, but decided that I liked this side of her immensely.

As Poppy rounded the corner to enter the kitchen, I picked up a gas mask from the counter and raised my eyebrows at her.

She laughed softly. "Connor picked that up for my birthday last year at a thrift store. He hates that chopping onions always makes me cry."

"Does it work?"

She shook her head. "Not even a little bit. But it was a sweet idea."

I set the gas mask down on the counter. "He's a good kid, Poppy. You've done a good job."

She smiled warmly, turning to greet Connor who had emerged from his bedroom with his shoes and jacket.

"Let's roll."

Chapter Sixteen

Poppy

"Connor," I shouted as I grabbed my keys. I walked over to his room, where I'd just helped him zip up his jacket, expecting him to follow me into the kitchen. When I walked into his astronaut-themed room he was in bed, clearly hiding under his spaceship comforter. I suppressed a laugh. I could tell he was trying not to breathe.

"Connor, we have to go," I said, walking over to the bed and pulling the covers off him. He'd only been home from school for a few minutes when I sprung this on him.

He furrowed his eyebrows.

"I don't need to go to the dentist. See…" He opened his mouth wide, revealing the gap in his front teeth where he'd lost another baby tooth.

I put my hands on my hips. "You have to go to the dentist. It's just a checkup. They want to make sure your big teeth will grow in right."

I groaned as I lifted him out of the bed and stood him up. "It will be quick, I promise. Let's go."

After getting Connor situated unhappily in the backseat of my car, I turned the key in the ignition, but it only made a puttering sound. I tried again, waiting for the engine to turn over, but it kept making the same sound.

"Come on," I muttered to myself.

"What's wrong? Can we not go?" Connor asked hopefully.

I tried one more time and the car spit out one last, loud putter and died.

Crap.

Between paying for school and only working part-time, the bills were already tight. I didn't need to look at my bank account to know that I couldn't afford even a minor car repair. I laid my head on the steering wheel, trying to gather myself so Connor wouldn't see how upset I was.

"It's okay, Mom," he said happily. "Now we can have fun instead of going to the dentist."

I smiled in spite of myself, lifting my head from the steering wheel. At least one of us was feeling positive about this.

Much to his excitement, I called and cancelled Connor's dentist appointment. I'd need to think of how to handle this situation, but until then I chose to put it out of my mind and focus on other things. In the spirit of optimism, I decided to use my now free afternoon to work on writing. I called my mom to see if she could watch Connor while I went to campus for the rest of the day. She had recently retired and jumped at any chance to get out of the house, especially if it involved spending time with her grandson. Within twenty minutes she was at my door.

"I can't believe this, what are you going to do about your car?" she said, breezing through the front door, her dark hair swept into a neat bun at the nape of her neck. She'd always been energetic, and when she entered a room it felt like the volume turned up a notch. I wasn't ready to discuss my car, since the whole thing was still making my head spin.

"I don't know yet. I'll figure something out," I said, hoping she'd drop it.

She shot me a look as she set a bag on the counter and started unloading groceries. Even though I'd told her a hundred times I didn't need her bringing us food she still couldn't resist.

"Don't give me that look," I said, smirking at her. She had a tendency to get worked up over every little thing, and even though this was kind of a big deal I knew it wouldn't help if she was stressed out about it.

"I'm sorry, Poppy, but you already have so much going on. You know, your dad and I could help you out," she said as she poured herself a cup of coffee.

I knew this was coming. They already did so much for Connor and me, and I hated to ask any more of them.

"It's okay, Mom, I'll be fine. I'll take care of it. I always figure it out, don't I?" She pursed her lips with anxiety. There was no convincing her at times like this. Instead of arguing with her, I gave her a quick hug, kissed Connor goodbye and ran out the door to catch the bus to campus.

I was only eight miles from campus, but the constant stopping and starting to pick up more students made it a forty-five-minute ride. I headed toward the building where most of the graduate writing students hung out in the writing lab during the day. As I reached for the door handle it opened from the other side and I walked straight into Zach. Our bodies bumped against each other lightly, and I reached out a hand to stop myself from fully bashing into him. It landed on his stomach, where I could feel his abs through the cotton of his button up. Our eyes met, and I was too aware of how near our mouths were. My lips parted, and I blinked rapidly, heat rushing through my body from being so close to him. I quickly pulled my hand away, hoping he hadn't noticed that I had let it linger for a few seconds longer than I really needed to.

"Poppy." He smirked. "In a rush?"

Get it together, I told myself. I had some serious lady-wood just from bumping into the guy. He grinned like he knew exactly what I was thinking.

"How's your day?" he asked as he stepped to the side, so we weren't blocking the doorway. "Have you fully recovered from your epic hangover yet?"

I ran my hands through my hair, taking a deep breath. I didn't really want to burden Zach with my problems but I couldn't lie to him, either.

"I've had better days," I admitted.

"Why? Did something happen?" Zach's tone was suddenly worried, and his green eyes flashed with concern.

"No, it's fine, it's just my car. It won't start." I waved a hand in the air, pretending I wasn't freaking out about it. "I'll figure it out."

"How are you getting around?"

I hadn't expected him to be so troubled by this. Taken aback, I shrugged. "The bus or Ubers, I guess."

"What about Connor?" Worry etched into his face. "I don't like the idea of you guys relying on the bus. Plus, it's getting colder. You can't be standing around waiting for a bus in these temperatures."

I couldn't help but frown a little. I didn't like him pointing out to me what I already knew. "Thanks for your concern, but I can handle it."

Unfazed by my brush-off, he continued, "Ubers aren't exactly safe either, have you seen those stories on the news?"

"You don't think I could take an Uber driver?" I grinned, trying desperately to keep things light. While it was nice of him to care so much, I was used to being independent so much so that his reaction made me uncomfortable.

"Come on, Poppy, I'm serious."

I sighed. Clearly, he wasn't going to let this go. "Sorry, it's just a tough situation. I'm short on money right now so I can't afford a repair. But seriously, the bus is fine."

As a young, single mother I'd made it through plenty of rough patches. Even if it meant eating ramen for a week and selling my couch, I intended to figure this out on my own.

"Seriously, you're sweet for caring." I smiled, trying to reassure him. "But you don't need to worry about it."

His green eyes were still lit up with his concern and his jaw flexed with anxiety. God, he even made stress look good. I swallowed, trying not to stare too much. How was it that even after a terrible day the sight of him still made my heart flutter?

I gestured inside. "I should probably get to work, but I'll see you around."

I left him standing uncertainly by the door. I could feel his gaze on me as I walked inside, but it wasn't the way he usually watched me, where I could practically feel him undressing me with his eyes. I hadn't expected a reaction like that; he was truly concerned about Connor and me. And even though I didn't need him to worry about me, I had to admit I was touched by his reaction.

* * *

After a long bus ride home, I wanted nothing more than to change into sweats and collapse on the couch with a tub of ice cream the size of my head. As I approached my duplex, I saw a truck parked behind my mom's Honda. When I got to the driveway, I read "Mike's Auto Repair" on the side of the truck. Then I noticed a pair of legs sticking out from under my car.

"Hello?" I said loudly.

The legs moved, and a man rolled out. He looked like he was about thirty years old, with short red hair.

"Hey." He grinned. "You're Poppy?"

I nodded, still unsure of what was happening. "No offense, but who are you and why are you under my car?"

"Mike." He gestured at his truck. Then he turned to look back at my car. "I had to replace the carburetor. And your brake pads don't look too great, either, so I'll go ahead and get those fixed up. I should be out of your hair soon."

He grinned, like the fact that he had appeared in my driveway and started fixing my car without my permission was totally normal. Figuring my mom had called him, I thanked him and barged inside. She knew I didn't like it when she got involved without asking me first.

"Mom," I shouted as I headed toward the living room. "Why did you call a—"

"Who's Zach?" she interrupted from the floor, where she was playing Legos with Connor.

"How do you know about..." I trailed off. *What the fuck is happening?* I could not have been more confused. "He's my adviser. Why?"

She shrugged, a knowing smile growing on her face. "You must be quite the student for him to call a repairman for you."

"Zach's my friend," Connor said, not taking his eyes off his Lego building. "He took us out for pancakes."

"Oh, really?" My mom asked innocently, her grin growing even wider. She was always trying to get me to date despite my repeatedly telling her I didn't have the time.

"What a nice adviser." She winked at me, putting up air quotes as she said adviser.

Now was not the time to get into my relationship with Zach, especially because I didn't even understand it myself. Wanting answers, I left them in the living room and walked back outside, where Mike was wiping his hands off with a greasy towel.

"So, Zach hired you?" I asked, trying to keep my voice even. I told him I was going to deal with it myself, why would he call a repairman for me? "I'm sorry but I can't really afford—"

Mike cut me off, putting his hands up. "Don't worry about payment. I'm an old friend of Zach's, and I owe him one. Probably more than one, honestly." He laughed.

I stood gaping as Mike loaded his tools into his truck.

"I'll need to come back once I get the right parts. I'm free in the morning, if that works."

I nodded, still stunned. *Zach did all this?* Mike climbed into his truck, then hesitated before closing the door. He grinned at me again. "He must really like you."

I smiled, not sure what to say, as he pulled the door shut. As I watched Mike's truck drive off, I still felt a slight tinge of annoyance that Zach had interfered with my life. I didn't want him thinking I couldn't take care of myself, or that I needed someone to swoop in and save me. Lost in my thoughts, I trudged back inside and sat on the couch, absentmindedly watching Connor play.

"What are you so grumpy about?" Mom asked. "Aren't you happy about your car?"

I looked up, not realizing I'd been so obvious. She could always see through to my true emotions, no matter how hard I tried to hide them.

"I just didn't need him to step in. I was handling it."

"Honey," she said gently, moving to sit next to me and putting a hand on my knee. "It's okay if you need help sometimes. It doesn't make you any less strong or less capable."

My mom and I might be totally different, but she always knew what to say. She gave my knee one last pat and stood up, heading into the kitchen where I could smell her famous lasagna baking. She turned back before rounding the corner.

"And if he's half as good looking as he is sweet, I'd say you need to hold onto this one."

"Mom, come on, he's just my adviser," I said, but I was grinning. She was right, it wasn't the worst thing in the world to get help sometimes, and accepting it was something I'd struggled with for a long time. I wanted to prove I could be the best mom to Connor and still achieve everything I wanted to in my life on my own. Even so, it was nice to have someone out there who cared enough to do this for me and Connor. The more I learned about Zach, the more I realized that even though his dirty mouth made it seem like he only cared about one thing, there was a lot more to him than sex. He was kind, caring, and thoughtful; a rare combination, if the guys I'd dated were any indication. I'm sure he saw some of his own mother in my struggles since he'd grown up with his mom his only parental support. And I was having a hard time ignoring what I hadn't wanted to admit for a long time. I was more than just attracted to Zach, I was really falling for him.

xo, Zach   235

Chapter Seventeen

Zach

Over the past few days, school had gotten busy and I hadn't seen much of Poppy, except for running into her on campus a couple of times. I'd texted her to let her know I was around if she needed help prepping for midterms. But after helping her get her car repaired, and her texted thank you, it seemed she had retreated for some space—thinking—but about what, I didn't know.

I had no choice but to give it to her, so I'd spent the last couple of days renovating my bedroom—beginning with sanding and staining the hardwood floor and repainting the walls a stone gray. Standing back to admire my work, I liked the finished affect. The white trim stood in stark contrast and the plain white sheets and down comforter I had seemed more elegant than before in the redesigned space.

It was late afternoon by the time I got all the paint and supplies put away in my garage and I was just stepping out of a warm shower when my doorbell rang. That was weird. I certainly wasn't expecting anyone on a

Saturday to show up unannounced.

Ducking into my bedroom, I grabbed a pair of jeans, and a t-shirt, opting to go commando in my rush to get to the door as the doorbell rang a second time.

"Coming," I called, buttoning my jeans just before pulling open the door.

It was Poppy.

She was dressed in a pair of black leggings and one of those oversized sweaters she seemed to love. This one was oatmeal colored and the hint of a lacy pink bra beneath was enough to make my cock twitch in my pants.

The way she stood on my front porch, expression open, hands relaxed at her sides, it gave nothing away. But then, she was here, wasn't she? It had to mean something.

"Come inside."

I took a step back and Poppy followed me in.

"You didn't have to do that," she said, turning to face me once we were inside my living room, her eyes blazing with that steely determination I loved. The energy crackling between us was something I'd become addicted to.

"Do what?"

"Fix my car."

I nodded. "I'm well aware of that. I wanted to, Poppy. I know you would have figured it out, but I didn't want you to have to do that for once."

She bit the inside of her cheek, thinking over what she wanted to say next. "So … you and Stacey … how's that whole thing going?"

She looked down at her boots and it took me a second to realize who she was talking about. The girl she saw me with at the bar.

I shrugged. "I wouldn't know. I haven't talked to her since Halloween. There's someone else I'm hung up on."

Poppy's eyes lifted to mine and her lips parted.

God, she was beautiful. Without any makeup, without all the fluff and frill society said women needed to be glamourous. Poppy just was. Full lips that trembled when she got nervous and eyebrows that would pinch together defiantly if she didn't like something I had to say.

"Oh?" she asked, that pretty mouth forming the word while her lip-gloss distracted me for what felt like the thousandth time.

Everything about this moment felt serendipitous, like we'd been building to this exact moment ever since we'd met at that party—a party we never should have been at—something so out of character for us both.

"Yeah." I stalked forward. I had no words. None. Zero. I stopped when I was inches from her, and staring down into those deliciously expressive eyes.

Poppy, of all people, deserved all the pretty words, all the whispered sweet phrases that ran through my brain at all hours, that I'd scrawled on scraps of paper and napkins, that I'd stuck inside of her bag. But the time for words was done. Lifting her chin with two fingers, I rubbed my thumb along those full, tempting lips. "If you tell me to stop, you better fucking mean it this time."

Poppy sucked in a sharp inhale, her eyes briefly falling closed before they blazed on mine once again. "First, I need to know your intentions."

I could have laughed. Could have fallen over right there in my living room. But I did neither of those things. *My intentions.* Was that what this was about? Was that why she stayed away? My intentions certainly weren't to fuck her and move on, I knew that much.

Apparently I needed to do a much better job at communicating with her, needed to lay out for Poppy exactly how I felt, exactly what I wanted.

But fuck, what did I want?

Did being with Poppy mean New York was off the table?

And how did I feel about that? Was I really okay with staying in this sleepy little town, advising students to live their dreams while I was too scared to live mine myself?

I took a deep, steadying breath. I wasn't sure I'd figure all of that out in the next few minutes, but I wasn't about to miss my shot with Poppy.

"I know you're incredible. I know you inspire me." I ran my thumb along her lower lip again. "I know I want you."

Her gaze darkened, and she looked as drunk with lust as I felt. "But what about after that, I'm not a one-night kind of girl, Zach…"

"I know that, Poppy. I've always known that. I want a shot with you. I always have."

She didn't say anything else. But she didn't have to. She lifted up on her toes, trying to close the height-difference between us and as adorable as her attempts were, I was done waiting. Placing my hands on her waist, I lifted Poppy from the floor, hauling her up to my chest. Our mouths crashed together as her legs crossed around my hips, and my hands moved to her ass. I held her there, held her against me, cherishing the weight of her, the feel of her soft breasts pressed against my chest, the sensation of her tongue moving with mine, the tiny whimpers she made when I thrust up experimentally to show her what she'd done to me.

"Zach." Poppy's mouth broke from mine, breathless and damp.

"Yes, beautiful, tell me what you want."

Her eyes were wild with want, her lips puffy and swollen from my kisses. For a moment, I thought she was going to demand I let her down, put an end to everything. But then she breathed a single word that ignited sparks inside my veins.

"You."

Rocking her up and down against my hard length, my

mouth attacked hers again. Still carrying her, I headed for my bedroom. Not bothering to break our kiss to look where I was going, I bumped us into the wall in the hallway and Poppy giggled against my mouth.

"Slow down, big guy. We've got all night."

I pulled back and met her eyes. "We do? But what about …"

Her smile was immediate. "Well, not *all* night, but Connor's at my parents' house for dinner. So we have a few hours at least."

Once inside my bedroom I set Poppy down, lowering her feet to the floor. I was happy that the scent of paint had mostly dissipated, and that I'd put everything back the way it was supposed to be. Poppy's eyes wandered around the room, before coming to rest on me once again. She took a deep breath, and then her fingers went to my belt, tugging, demanding.

Looking down, I watched her slender fingers unlatch my belt and unsnap the button. Then she was pushing her hands inside my jeans.

"Fuck," I growled, pushing my fingers into my hair, and resting my hands on top of my head.

"Where are your underpants, Mr. Austin?" She made a low sound of disapproval under her breath. But then she drew out my cock, now fully hard, and sucked in a sharp inhale, the noise of surprise dying in her throat. "Shit. Zach."

A slow smile uncurled on my lips. "Yes, Poppy?"

"Your dick is like really fucking big."

I ran one finger slowly down her cheek and pride and heat dueled inside my chest. "Hmm. A smart girl like you, an English lit major no less, surely you can think of a better adjective than *big*?"

I was enjoying this way too much. But my dick hadn't been touched by anyone other than me in a long time, and this wasn't just anyone—this was Poppy, who I'd fantasized about nonstop for weeks on end. And now she was here, in my bedroom, curling her delicate fist around my wide shaft and giving it an experimental tug. Pleasure burst through every cell in my body.

"It's ... God. It's so hot, Zach. I want you."

Without another word, Poppy dropped to her knees on the wood floors I'd so painstakingly refinished all the while trying not to think about her. In the next breath, she brought those sexy pink-glossed lips to the head of my cock. Her tongue licked languidly across my wide tip and down the side of my shaft. I thought I might explode then and there.

"Is this okay?" She peered up at me through her eyelashes, teasing.

"Yes, yes. Please." I cupped her cheek and Poppy opened wider, the head of my cock disappearing inside the warm, wet heat of her mouth.

"Fuck that feels good," I groaned.

While Poppy worked me over, both with her mouth and her hands, I focused on trying not to come down her pretty little throat.

My own personal temptress, the fire of my loins.

"So good, so good, sweetheart."

Poppy made a noise of want in her throat, swallowing me farther.

Every wicked and depraved fantasy I'd dared not to harbor came bursting to brilliant life.

Knowing that I was only moments away from losing control, I pulled Poppy from my cock, and hauled her to her feet. Kissing her swollen lips, I worked on stripping her of every last article of clothing until she stood naked before me.

Flushed pale skin, shapely hips, full tits with pretty blush-colored nipples. She was beautiful and I told her so.

Blushing, she crawled onto my bed and waited while I pushed down my jeans and stripped off my t-shirt.

When I laid on top of her, I finally understood what those ancient poets had meant about hearing doves cry, and angels sing and all that shit—because fuck. The heat of her silky, naked skin pressed up against mine was enough to send me straight down onto one knee. I never wanted this moment to end, never wanted Poppy to leave my bed, and the few precious hours we had wouldn't be nearly enough.

I rolled to my side and Poppy did the same, our hands, our mouths refusing to leave each other's bodies for long.

She stroked my cock with both hands, while I played with her pussy, learning what she liked until I'd made her come twice by rubbing her clit.

"Condoms," she breathed. "Please tell me you have

condoms."

I wanted to fuck her, wanted to bury myself balls-deep inside her and never leave. But Poppy's words kept ringing in my ears. She wasn't a one and done type of girl. And before I claimed her, she was right. I needed to know what my intentions were with this beautiful single mother who'd stormed into my life and staked claim to my heart.

I pressed a kiss to her forehead. "Not tonight. I don't want to rush it."

A smile blossomed on her lips right before she crawled down my body and pushed me flat on my back. Then her lips closed over me again, and nothing else mattered.

The sweet little Poppy Ellis who'd fought this every step of the way, was sucking me like her very life depended on it and I was lost.

Chapter Eighteen

Poppy

I practically ran out of class, pulling on my coat and scarf as I went. Zach's office was in the building, and with our track record I knew if I stuck around too long I'd be sure to run into him. As if on cue, he stepped out of an office down the hall. I made a quick turn and darted around a corner, hoping he hadn't seen me. I waited, listening for his footsteps. After a few moments of silence, I peered around the corner; he was gone. *What the hell am I doing?* I was a graduate student and a mom, and here I was cowering behind a wall to avoid a guy. What was wrong with this picture?

I'd been avoiding Zach ever since I went to thank him for fixing my car. That night I let my emotions, and my libido, get the best of me. I'd never expected to feel the way I did about him, but I still didn't see how we could be together and I worried I was leading him on. I shouldn't have let things go so far. It was a moment of weakness; I was only human, right? Ever since then I'd been ignoring his texts, and I was sure my mixed signals weren't going over well.

The problem was, he was moving to New York. And even if he wasn't … there were no guarantees we could work. Absolutely none, so I was trying not to focus on it.

I headed toward the Daily Grind, a cozy little coffee shop near campus, where I was meeting Kody and Jodee to study. We were in the middle of mid-terms, and I had a new paper due at the end of the week.

"Hey, girl." Kody grinned at me from behind his laptop.

Jodee was hunched over, her laptop open, with a huge stack of papers next to it. We were seated near the door, and every time it opened a burst of cold air would come in, making Jodee shiver dramatically. She was so focused she hadn't even looked up when I walked in.

I set my things down on the table and waved a hand near Jodee's face. "Hey, are you okay? We can move to a different table."

She finally noticed me with a start.

"Oh, sorry, no it's fine. I just have to read all these stories people submitted for the literary journal. And I haven't even started revising my own poems."

I had nearly forgotten that Jodee was the Assistant Editor at the school literary journal, which meant she had to read almost every story and poem that was submitted on top of her own academic workload.

"I keep telling her she's going to break her back hunching over like that all day." Kody shook his head.

I gave Jodee a sympathetic look, but she was already back in her own world. I decided it was best not to bother her again.

"Are you almost done with your poems?" I asked Kody after I'd ordered my usual coffee.

"Close. What about you?"

"I've barely started," I sighed. Between shuttling Connor between school and football practice and working part-time I'd hardly had time to even think about my course work.

I put in my headphones, selecting the opera that I liked to listen to while I wrote. I really needed to focus on revising, but every time the door of the Daily Grind opened a bell rang and I would turn around anxiously. I knew I was being slightly ridiculous, but it wouldn't surprise me if Zach wandered in here and I didn't want him sneaking up on me.

"What's with you? You're all jumpy," Kody asked through a mouthful of blueberry muffin.

I hesitated. I knew if I told him I was afraid of Zach walking through the door I'd sound slightly crazy. Then again, they'd seen me in some pretty crazed moments and never judged me.

I shrugged. "It's not a big deal, I just don't really want to run into Zach right now."

"Typical." Kody gave me a dubious look. "Can you just bone him already so we can stop playing these games?"

I felt myself going red. I hadn't told either of them what had happened between Zach and me, mostly because I didn't know how I felt about it myself. Kody noticed my face and narrowed his eyes.

"Hold on, did you two finally go to pound town?"

Jodee looked up from the story she'd been studying.

I wrinkled my nose. "Gross, and no. But we did… other stuff."

"Oh my God," Kody shouted, causing most of the

coffee shop to turn and stare at us. He and Jodee grinned at each other so excitedly I half expected them to high five. Kody lowered his voice. "So you got a preview? That's smart, you should always test drive before you buy." He clapped his hands. "This is the best day of my life."

I grinned. "I think you need to reevaluate your life experiences if that's true."

"Don't change the subject. So when are you going to finally seal the deal?" He was talking a mile a minute. "Wait, why are you avoiding him? Was it bad?" He whispered the last sentence, seemingly horrified at the prospect.

"No way," Jodee jumped in, turning to me. "He's too perfect. It wasn't bad, was it?"

I put up my hands, trying to slow them down. "Don't worry. It was…" I searched for the right word. "Amazing."

But amazing didn't even begin to describe it. Life changing was more like it. My skin prickled just talking about it.

"But he's still my adviser, and that isn't changing

anytime soon. I just feel like we should have thought about it more before we did anything physical."

"Girl, all you do is think." Kody waved his hand in the air like he could wave away my concerns. "You need to live your life."

Jodee nodded seriously. "I know I told you not to go for it before, but I feel like you actually really like each other."

I smiled uneasily. Maybe they were right, but still the thought of having to sneak around was exhausting. And I didn't even want to think about the consequences if we were caught.

Luckily, we had so much work to do we didn't have time to discuss my relationship with Zach any further. After several more hours and too many coffees, I vibrated back to my car. As I searched for my keys I felt the smooth paper of the latest poem that had been left in my bag. I pulled it out and read it, smiling. I'd never been a huge fan of love poems, but something about these were different. They felt so personal.

I still hadn't figured out who was leaving them, despite my best snooping. I'd purposely left my bag unattended in class and watched out of the corner of my eye, but nobody had taken the bait. While this wasn't exactly Sherlock Holmes-level investigating, I still couldn't understand how I hadn't noticed who was leaving them. Zach flashed through my mind. Could it be him? He'd certainly had enough opportunities alone with me to slip something into my bag. But still, it seemed impossible. These poems were sweet and tender, which was so not his style. He was crass and straightforward; there was no way poems like these could come from him.

* * *

That night, Connor's school was throwing their fall dance. The "dance" was mostly a random assortment of games and activities with a local DJ playing music in the corner. Connor was especially excited about the cake walk, which I'd had to practically drag him away from last year. This year, he won on his third try and chose a pan of frosted brownies as his prize. While I wasn't especially enthusiastic about him stuffing himself with brownies so close to bedtime, he was so excited that I couldn't say no.

"Poppy," a voice shouted from across the room. It was Sandra, the mom of Connor's best friend, Jordan.

I smiled, waving her over. I had always liked Sandra.

Unlike some of the other parents, she'd never judged me for being young or a single mother. Plus, she always had so much energy and a smile on her face, which was a welcome sight in a crowd of parents I didn't know.

"How's school?" she asked as Connor and Jordan compared prizes. "Have you met anyone interesting there?" She gave a small wink as she said interesting.

I laughed uncomfortably. "It's great, I love the program. Everyone is really nice."

As much as I liked Sandra, there was no way I was confessing to her that not only had I almost slept with my adviser but, that I was receiving random love poems from an anonymous wordsmith.

We continued to catch up while the boys got involved in a boisterous game of Twister. I hadn't realized how uncomfortable I'd been before Sandra showed up. The other parents were nice, but distant. I think they weren't sure how to socialize with someone who was so much younger than them and unmarried. Whenever we came to school events it was painfully obvious that Connor was the only kid without a dad. Even the divorced parents seemed to find a way to both show up.

When he was younger, he'd ask me why his dad never came, but after a few years he'd gotten used to it. Still, I knew it had to be on his mind, and I always felt a little twinge of guilt about it.

Connor ran over and grabbed onto my shirt. "Mom, can I have tickets to do the cake walk again? Please?"

I glanced at Sandra, and she gave me a knowing smile. Jordan wanted to keep playing Twister, so we agreed to meet back up later in the night. As Connor pulled me forward, I felt my phone buzzing in my pocket. I stopped in my tracks when I saw the caller ID.

Zach was calling. I stared at it for a few seconds, too nervous to make any movement in case it would somehow answer the call. He usually just texted, but he must have been wondering why I'd been ignoring his texts. I just wasn't ready to talk about what had happened between us yet. More than that, I worried that if I was alone with him I wouldn't be able to stop myself from doing it again, and more. The memory had come back in random flashes since that night, and just the thought of it sent a rush of heat straight to my lady bits and made my heart pick up a few paces. I could practically come just from thinking about his tongue on my nipples, running along my body and down to my… *Get a grip, Poppy, you're around children.* I forced thoughts of Zach from my mind and turned my phone off, but not before realizing that Connor had seen the name on the screen.

"When is Zach coming over again?" he asked, tugging on my arm to get me walking again.

Shit. I really needed an exit strategy to handle this.

"I'm not sure," I said carefully. I didn't realize how much Connor would like him after just one meeting, and I definitely didn't want my son getting hurt because I couldn't control myself around Zach. "We're both really busy."

"Next time he comes over he can help me build my Lego castle."

I bit my lip, not sure what to say. I had to admit, the image of Zach on the floor with Connor building a Lego castle was pretty adorable.

"We'll see if he has time." I gave Connor's hand a squeeze, worried that I'd made an even bigger mess of things than I'd realized.

In the crowd of happy families, it was hard not to

want that for Connor and for myself if I was being honest. I tried to be both a mom and a dad for him, but it would definitely be nice to have a positive male role model in his life. Zach was sweet and thoughtful, had a great career, and he had been great with Connor. It was all too easy to imagine the three of us on the weekends, cooking breakfast together in the kitchen or taking Connor to play in the park. I didn't know what would happen between Zach and me, but I knew I'd better figure it out fast because I was in way deeper than I'd ever expected.

Chapter Nineteen

Zach

~~Your words are your testimony, and I've become a believer.~~

~~I didn't think it was possible, but your inner beauty has surpassed your outer.~~

~~Where you go, I want to follow.~~

I crumpled the piece of paper into a ball and tossed it across my office where it landed with a satisfying swish into the wastepaper basket. My words weren't enough. Nothing would ever be enough.

One magical night spent in my arms wasn't enough to persuade the ever-cautious Poppy to give me a real shot. We'd spent a few perfect hours in my bed doing everything but making love, and now I was a believer.

I'd gone and done the stupidest thing I could think of, I'd fallen for her—a student, a woman who'd claimed to have sworn off men—and a single mom. I knew nothing about parenting, knew nothing about the commitments that might come with dating someone who was a mother, but none of that mattered. I wanted to try.

And I was willing to face whatever consequences the university might throw my way. But was Poppy?

I tore out a fresh sheet of paper, took a deep breath, then tried again.

Poppy,

You're scared—and so am I, but I'm not too afraid to try. You've told me all the reasons why we're wrong for each other. But let me tell you some of the reasons why we'd be perfect together.

I feel more for you in the past few weeks than I have for anyone—in years. You said you were looking for someone smart, someone funny. You also said you'd prefer that person have a vagina, but let's be honest, Poppy. ~~You sucked on my dick like it was a popsicle on the Fourth of July.~~

The obstacles you've faced and overcome only make you more beautiful in my eyes. I adore Connor and while I'd take things as slow as you wanted, I'd love to be part of his life too.

I've fallen completely in love with you. It's wrong, I know. I'm an advisor—you're a student. But I couldn't live with myself if I didn't put my truth out there and at least try.

And if that's not enough, I promise you will always come first, and that I will chop all your onions. Forever and ever.

What do you say? Be mine?

xo, Zach

I stared down at the words on the page. They were honest, raw. I'd laid myself bare, and I had no idea what Poppy's response might be, but I couldn't live with myself if I never tried.

Folding the note into thirds, I slid it into an envelope, and sealed it, quickly scrawling Poppy's name on the outside.

Then I checked my calendar, and chewed on my lip as I evaluated if I had enough time to deliver the letter to her house over my lunch break.

Fuck it.

So, I'd probably be a few minutes late. Poppy was worth it. She was worth everything.

By the time I arrived back at the office, I only had time to grab a cup of coffee and a stale bagel from the faculty lounge, but it didn't matter. My appetite was gone. I hadn't been brave enough to ring her doorbell, to deliver the letter myself, so even though her car was parked in the drive, I'd stuck the envelope in her mailbox and sped away, like a pathetic teenager with an unrequited crush. But the truth was, I wasn't brave enough to watch her read it, wasn't brave enough to be rejected.

I took a sip of my coffee and tried to focus on work. A sudden knock at my door had my stomach knotting with nerves. Was it Poppy?

I rose and pulled open the door.

"Hi, Mr. Austin." The geeky looking kid who always wore pajama pants grinned up at me.

"Hey, Tad. What's up?"

He swallowed, looking nervous. He'd never been to see me during my office hours before, and I wondered what was on his mind. Whatever it was, maybe it'd be a good distraction from what was on mine.

"I was hoping you could look over my paper for Dr. Chan. See if it's up to her standards."

"Sure thing. Come in." I stepped aside, wandering back to my desk and waited while he pulled out the single page double-spaced essay he'd written.

While I read over his paper, Tad played on his phone. I didn't get young people's fascination with their phones. Like they couldn't go three seconds without reaching for the damn things. I realized that Poppy had never done that. I'd never once seen her fill a quiet moment by staring at a screen. It was just one more thing I liked about her.

I finished the paper, and pulled out a red pen.

"May I?" I asked.

Tad nodded, and stuffed his phone back inside his pocket.

"This opening line could be stronger for starters. It needs a hook. Needs to give the reader a reason to care, a strong pull to read on."

He nodded, brows pushing together.

I reworked his first line, and Tad nodded eagerly.

"Wow. Thanks."

I continued going over my feedback on how to improve the piece and was just about finished when someone else knocked on my door.

Tad grabbed the page, and rose to his feet. "I think I can take it from here. Thanks again. I see now why Poppy has said such great things about you."

I smirked, heading for the door. "Poppy has?"

He nodded. "Yeah, a bunch of times, actually."

Hope bloomed in my chest, and as I opened the door to my office, somehow, I already knew who would be standing there.

She was here.

Tad let himself out, turning sideways to scoot around her.

If he suspected something, he didn't show it. And seconds later, he was gone, disappearing down the hall and leaving the woman I'd fallen for standing just an arm's length away.

When I looked back at Poppy, I saw for the first time there were unshed tears in her eyes.

"It was you," she whispered.

The poems. She must have recognized my handwriting. I nodded.

"I knew it was you." A single tear rolled down her cheek, and I took her hand, tugging her inside my office and closing the door behind us.

"But I don't understand, what about New York?" she asked, eyes wide and glued to mine.

"Fuck New York, Poppy."

"What do you mean fuck New York? It's your dream. I won't let you give that up for me."

I shook my head, trying to put my thoughts in order. "I thought I needed a change of scenery, thought I needed to go somewhere to leave this writer's block behind. It turns out I was just looking for inspiration from the wrong place, or writing the wrong fucking book entirely. My fiction project wasn't coming together no matter how hard I tried to force it. And then I realized why. Nothing between us has been fiction, Poppy. Nothing has been fake. From that first moment you asked me to be your fake date—we both knew. We felt it then. It scared you, but you can't deny it. We have a connection. It's big and it's real and it scares me too, Poppy."

Her lower lip trembled, and she drew a steadying breath. "What are you saying, Zach? You don't want to go to New York anymore?"

I shook my head. "These past few days, I've started a new manuscript—nonfiction. The story of us, and it's flowing from me like nothing else has before. I don't need to go to New York. Not when my muse is right here."

"I would never ask you to do that," she said, voice breathless.

"You don't have to. I'm insisting on it. The only way I'm moving anywhere is if you and Connor come with me, but for now, I'm staying put."

With tears still shining in her eyes, Poppy reached for my hand. "So, tell me about the story of us. Is there a happy ending?"

I chuckled and gave her hand a squeeze. "I'm not that far yet, but yes, I can promise you there will be. There's so much sex though, it's ridiculous." I was kidding, but my words had the desired effect. Poppy raised her eyebrows and let out a soft laugh.

"Is that so, Mr. Austin?"

My mouth captured hers in a fiery kiss, and within seconds, I was lifting her, setting her on the edge of my desk where I could worship her mouth with mine. Nipping at her lower lip, she parted her lips for me, granting me the entrance I sought.

Fingers tugged at buttons and belts and our kisses grew hot. But after only a few minutes, the reality of our setting slammed into me like a ton of bricks. I pulled back and straightened her sweater.

"Come home with me Poppy. Make love to me. Be mine." I met her eyes with determination. She couldn't reject me now. She wouldn't. I could feel it.

She smoothed one hand over my hair where her roaming fingers had made a mess of it. "You really promise to chop all my onions? That's a big task."

"I meant every word I said in that letter."

She pressed her lips to mine once again. "I have one more lecture I need to attend today. Then I'll pick up Connor from school and bring him to my parents' house for the night."

"All night?"

She nodded. "I think we'll need some time to figure things out, don't you?"

The only things I intended to figure out tonight was if she liked it fast and deep or slow and tender, but I nodded. "We do."

"I'll see you at six?" she asked.

"I'll make dinner. See you then."

With one last, chaste kiss Poppy was gone.

* * *

Why the fuck had I said I would make dinner? It was no secret that I didn't really know how to cook—save for throwing a steak on the grill or warming myself something in the microwave.

At five o'clock I grabbed my phone, resigned that I would just order a pizza. But then it occurred to me I didn't know what Poppy liked on her pizza, and I really didn't want to fuck tonight up by something so mundane as the wrong pizza toppings. So instead I dialed the one person I knew would help me.

"Hello?"

"Hey, Mom."

"Hi, honey. What's going on?"

"Poppy's coming over for dinner in an hour and I have no idea what to make."

My mother let out a joyful squeal that caused me to pull the phone back from my ear. "Oh, there's so many wonderful things you could make. I can come over and help …"

"No, Mom. I've got this." The last thing I wanted Poppy to find when she got here was my mom and me stirring pots and bickering when she arrived.

Mom hummed something to herself. "Fine. What do you have in terms of ingredients?"

I opened my fridge, and after surveying the inspiring contents, I opened the freezer next. "Frozen chicken breast and some cheese. And beer."

"She'll be there in an hour you said?"

"Yeah." My gut tensed and for a second I thought I was fucked.

"I'll tell you what. I just made homemade pizza dough for my dinner. What if I brought you that?"

I could have laughed at the irony if I wasn't so stressed. Far be it from me to argue with the universe's plan that we eat pizza tonight. "I don't know what she likes on her pizza."

Mom huffed. "I've got everything. Pepperoni, mushrooms, spinach, pesto, olives, you name it."

Shit. That would be awesome. "You would do that?

What will you eat?"

"For my one and only son? You bet I would. And I'll figure it out. It's not a big deal, Zachary."

"Thanks, Mom."

"'Course, sweetie. I'll be there in fifteen minutes to drop everything off."

After I hung up, I did have a moment where I felt like a douchebag for needing my mom to bail me out tonight.

But then she arrived with the dough and ingredients, and even a bottle of red wine, and I let all that go.

I gave her a kiss on the cheek. "Thanks, this is perfect."

"I know." Mom smiled and without any fanfare, she turned and headed back to her car. I'd been half-worried that she'd try to wrestle her way into my dinner with Poppy, and was relieved to see her drive away.

Soon I had two lopsided pizza crusts rolled out onto sheet pans and the wine opened and resting. All that was left to do was wait.

I had no idea which way tonight was going to go—

would Poppy say yes to this, to me? Or would she reject my offer and leave me brokenhearted?

Chapter Twenty

Poppy

I held up a pair of black panties, biting my lip. I'd spent the last twenty minutes staring at underwear, trying to pick out the perfect pair. I'd been a bundle of excited nerves all afternoon, my heart alternating between skipping lightly and pounding when I thought about what I was about to do.

I chose a black, lacy thong with a matching bra and tiptoed into the bathroom. Earlier, I'd dropped Connor off at my parents' house, where he was spending the night. Rather than admitting I was going out to get laid, I had told my parents I was meeting up with someone from school to work on writing and would probably be out late. It was almost true, right?

After I'd shaved and moisturized, I carefully applied eye liner, mascara, and a nude lipstick. I smiled in the mirror to check the effect, and my stomach fluttered. I couldn't believe I was going to spend the night at Zach's. It was more than that though – I couldn't believe I was actually going to pursue the idea of actually being with him. I kept grinning as I walked back to the bedroom to get dressed. I was still in shock that he was the one leaving those poems, but I guess I should have known. He was so sweet and caring, and well, his dirty mouth was just a small part of who he was.

I pulled on tights and a black dress that was a bit more snug than I usually went for. I looked in the mirror, adjusting my dark hair. I slipped into a pair of black heeled boots and smiled at myself one more time in the mirror before making the drive to Zach's place.

* * *

As I rang the doorbell, my heart began to pound. I hadn't expected to be nervous, but sleeping with the sexiest, smartest, most caring man I'd ever met, who also happened to be my graduate adviser? I wasn't exactly a virgin, but this was definitely uncharted territory.

The door swung open and my breath caught in my chest, the combination of my nerves and excitement making the sight of Zach all the more jarring. He looked as sexy as always, in black jeans and a button up plaid shirt. His hair was messier than usual, and I couldn't help thinking of how I'd be running my hands through it later. I swallowed at the thought, forcing it from my head.

"Hey," I said, as I stepped inside, grinning stupidly. My mind felt blank. I was acting like a teenager about to get her first kiss. I swallowed and grinned at him, hoping he didn't notice my nerves.

"Hey," he said, grinning back, running a hand through his hair. "Come on in."

He gestured inside, but he seemed less forward than usual. Was it possible that Zach, crass, dirty mouth Zach, was just as nervous as I was?

I set my bag down and felt Zach watching me from the doorway.

He crossed the room toward me, and helped me out of my coat before hanging it in the hall closet. When he turned to look at me in my dress, he let out a low groan.

"Fuck. You look so damn sexy right now."

Suddenly he was across the room, all shyness gone, pulling me against him and kissing me roughly. He backed me up against the wall as I parted my lips in surprise. I was taken aback for a moment before my instincts kicked in, and I unbuttoned his shirt until I could slide my hands along his bare chest and stomach. There was no one here to discover us—I could be as bold as I never dared before.

But Zach had another idea and he grabbed my hands and pinned them to the wall, pressing his body against mine so that I could feel his erection through his pants. I gasped as he roughly kissed my neck and I fought to free my hands so I could grab onto him, but he held me in place, making my heart race.

He stopped kissing me and looked at me, his deep emerald eyes hazy with desire, which turned me on even more.

"You want me to slow down?" he asked.

"And ruin all my fun?" I said, feeling cheeky.

Zach let out a sound that was somewhere between a grunt and a growl and either way, it was the sexiest noise I'd ever heard. Letting go of my hands, he grabbed my hips and lifted me in the air. I wrapped my legs around him and he continued to kiss my neck and shoulders as he walked us to his bedroom.

Once inside, he tossed me onto the bed, pulling his shirt the rest of the way off, before focusing his attention back on me. Looking at me with adoration and wonder, Zach lifted my dress off over my head, and then dropped to his knees before me, like I was an altar and he came to worship me. Removing each boot and setting it aside, Zach carefully began to pull down my tights, dragging his fingers along my thighs as he went. My skin tingled with anticipation, and heat rocketed through me. When he was finished slipping off my tights, he rose to his feet again. The room was completely still and silent, except for the pounding of my heart.

"Are you sure about this? I need to be certain this is what you want." His voice was a low, sexy growl.

"I'm sure." I'd never been more sure of anything in my entire life.

Zach pulled off his jeans, revealing the outline of his very hard cock through his boxer briefs. If I wasn't wet before, now I was soaking. I'd dreamed of his body—of this particular appendage since we were last together. And tonight I'd finally have him in all the ways I'd fantasized about.

He climbed onto the bed, dragging me closer to him. I arched my back and moaned softly when I felt him rub against me. He slowly peeled off my panties, dragging his fingers along my body like he had with the tights, making me writhe with desire. When I was completely bare, I reached for his boxer briefs, my fingers shaking like a nervous child unwrapping her Christmas present too early.

"God, you make me crazy," he groaned as my fingertips grazed his bare skin. I continued tugging until his cock sprang free—it was perfect, and even bigger than I remembered.

The sight of it made me crave him all the more, made my desire jump to new heights, and I let out a shaky breath and reached for him, ready to feel him inside me, but Zach had other plans.

"Turn over," he breathed.

I was breathing heavily, my pulse thundering loudly in my ears, so caught up in how much I wanted him that it took me a moment to register what he'd said. I was so full of need for him I would have done anything he asked me to. I turned over, nervously waiting for what he planned to do to me. Zach ran his hands along my hips and grabbed my ass in his hands. Then he gave it a hard slap, making me cry out. I arched my back again, lifting it toward him, and before it had even stopped stinging he slapped my tender flesh again. He kissed up and down my spine, making my body tremble, every nerve on high alert. Each time he kissed me I moaned, my breath coming in short gasps. He took his time, stroking my skin, kissing and nibbling everywhere he could reach. I felt worshipped, like a goddess. A goddess who was in heat. As he moved up to kiss my shoulders, his hand slid down my spine.

My heart sped up and I whimpered as he slipped his fingers into the wetness between my legs. He rubbed me back and forth, gently touching my clit each time. My hips began to rock as I let out low moans, until I knew I needed to feel him inside me. I tried to turn over, but he held me down, continuing to rub me, before sliding his fingers roughly inside of me.

"Zach," I moaned.

My heart was beating out of my chest and I could feel that I was close to coming. Just when I was about to lose control, he pulled his hand away and turned me over onto my back. Staring into my eyes, he reached a hand down to start fingering me again, but before he could I reached forward and grabbed onto his erection. He paused, letting out a low groan. I rubbed the length of him, ready to take control, guiding him toward me and rubbing his cock along the wetness between my legs.

"Fuck, Poppy," he muttered as I rocked my hips against him. "Be a good girl, and let me get you ready."

Trying to draw him closer, Zach grabbed my hand, pinning my arms above my head like he had earlier. He kissed my neck again, then moved down my chest, his tongue dancing circles around my nipple. I whimpered, my back arching toward him. Gazing up at me, he slid his tongue over my nipple, making me cry out, then gently bit down on it. I continued to moan as he moved onto the other breast, still pinning my wrists down to the bed, making me ache between my legs.

I couldn't wait any longer. I wrapped my legs around him and pulled his hips closer to mine, hoping to urge him inside. He let go of my wrists and bent down to kiss me. As his tongue moved into my mouth, dancing along my tongue, he put his hand up to my breasts, rubbing both nipples at once. I slid my hands up his arms and into his hair, grabbing onto it in a fist as I arched my back and bit his lip. I kept my legs wrapped around him, until the tip of him rubbed against my clit again, sending desire scorching through me.

"Please fuck me," I whimpered, which was all the encouragement he needed. He sat up, quickly sheathed himself in a condom, and grabbed onto my hips with both hands.

And then it was like all time stopped. Zach pressed another soft kiss to my mouth, then another, before pulling back to meet my eyes.

"Are you sure? If you've changed your mind, if any of this doesn't feel right, just say the word..."

I shook my head. "I want you. I've always wanted you."

The hint of a smile twitched on his mouth. "And I, you, sweetheart."

Positioning himself between my thighs, Zach pushed forward until I felt the broad head of him nudging against my labia. I let out a long exhale, and slowly, so slowly, Zach slid himself inside of me, inch by inch.

I cried out, thrusting my hips up toward him.

His hand low on my pubic bone stopped me. "Wait."

"I want it." He was huge, but still I wanted him fully

inside of me.

"And you shall have it."

I moaned softly as he continued to move maddeningly slow, gently thrusting himself in and out of me, sinking in deeper each time. Just before he was fully inside, he pulled out completely. I reached for him, shocked by the sudden feeling of emptiness.

"Your pussy feels so good," he whispered, then pushed himself inside of me, roughly this time. I dug my nails into his shoulders as he thrust faster and harder. His breathing was coming out in gasps. I was moaning loudly, totally consumed by desire. Every nerve in my body felt electrified and I could hardly breathe. I dug my nails harder into his shoulders as my mind went blank and I finally let go, crying out loudly, my body finally giving into everything I'd denied it.

Moving one hand between us, Zach rubbed careful, teasing circles over my clit as his strokes grew more firm.

"Fuck, you are …" He didn't finish that sentence, but the low groan that escaped him, and his powerful hips pummeling into me made me lose my mind.

My muscles contracted, I came in wave after

maddening wave of pleasure that seemed to go on and on.

Zach fucked me slowly, letting me ride the delicious swells of pleasure, his gaze lowering to watch where his flesh so lewdly speared into mine.

"So sexy. So good."

"You too," I groaned, finally able to form words.

I couldn't help my brain from jumping to the realization that Zach was all man—far from some adolescent who couldn't control his body—and he'd waited for me to come first, before he started pumping his hips in earnest, chasing his own release.

Finally, I knew he was close when the muscles in his shoulders stiffened and he let out a satisfied groan, emptying himself inside me.

Zach didn't move, still inside me as we continued to breathe heavily. He looked into my eyes for a moment before he gently kissed me on the forehead and moved so he was lying next to me, turning his head to examine his shoulder where I'd been digging my nails into it.

"Are you going to do that every time? I might need to wear some padding." He smirked.

I slapped him playfully, grinning. "I didn't hear any complaints."

He turned on his side, propping his head up with his arm, allowing me the view of all that sexy muscle and ink.

"Seriously, though, that was pretty fucking amazing." He started drawing circles on my stomach with his other hand, which made me shiver. I swallowed. How was I already turned on again? "Maybe I should sleep with students more often."

I snorted. "Are you trying to get even more injuries?"

"Only if they're from you." He grinned, pushing the hair from my face. He kissed me, and I moved closer to him, so our bodies were nestled together. He kissed me deeply, as if it knew this would be a perfect moment to ruin, my stomach let out a loud growl. He pulled back and we both started laughing.

"I know how this goes." Zach laughed, rolling over to get out of bed. "We better get you something to eat ASAP."

I stayed in bed, watching him as he stood and stretched, feeling relieved that there was no post-sex awkwardness between us. I was still processing that I'd finally had sex with Zach, and it was even better than I could have imagined. He turned and noticed me staring, and for once I didn't look away. He grinned, bent down and kissed me, then gave my butt a light slap.

"I need to feed you. You're going to need the energy for what I've got planned later."

I grinned, rolling out of bed. Not wanting to put on my whole get-up again, I borrowed an over-sized t-shirt emblazoned with our college logo and a pair of drawstring shorts from Zach. He was pulling ingredients from the refrigerator when I walked into the kitchen, and when he turned and saw me he let out a low whistle.

"I would never have thought that outfit could be sexy, but you pull it off."

I laughed, coming around the counter to examine what he was making. There was homemade pizza dough and all the ingredients laid out on the counter.

"You like pizza?" he asked.

I nodded. "I love it. This is actually perfect. Connor and I order pizza every Friday night. But making it sounds like even more fun."

Zach nodded, handing me a jar of sauce. "We can all

three make it together sometime."

I liked the idea of that, but didn't want to get ahead of myself.

We busied ourselves topping our pies with tomato sauce and various toppings. And after setting the timer for the oven, we retreated to the living room with glasses of red wine in hand.

When the pizza was ready, we ate casually, sitting at the kitchen table across from one another. We chatted while we ate, and it felt so natural to be with him like this, I wondered how I'd fought against it for so long.

"Is there anything you aren't good at?" I asked, carrying our empty plates to the sink when we were finished.

"Self-control?" he asked, pulling me toward him as I walked back toward the table. He leaned forward to kiss me, but I put a hand out to stop him. Summoning my courage, I pulled the drawstring on the shorts, letting them drop to the floor and then pulled off his t-shirt so I was standing naked in front of him. His eyes travelled along my body and I shivered like he'd actually touched me, feeling my nipples harden, heat shooting between my legs at the look of desire on his face. I straddled him in his chair, leaning down to kiss him. He reached a hand for my breast, but I stopped him, pushing his hand back down.

"Not yet." I smiled. I heard his breathing grow heavier as I kissed his neck, then pulled his own shirt off and dropped it onto the floor. I bent lower, running my tongue along his hard chest and across his nipple. He breathed in, reaching a hand to grip onto my hair, but I pushed it away, smiling up at him.

I moved so I was kneeling on the floor in front of him as I unbuttoned his jeans, pulling them and his boxer briefs down as he lifted his hips, revealing his rock hard nine inches. I looked up at him, meeting his emerald eyes before I started to lick the tip of his erection. His abs tightened, and he groaned as I put my mouth around the head, continuing to move my tongue along him, slowly taking more of him in my mouth. I moved up and down, wrapping a hand around his shaft, pausing at the tip to run my tongue along it. He let out a low sound, almost a growl, and I felt myself getting wet. I took him in even deeper, and his breathing grew more labored. He put a hand on my head, gripping my hair in his fist, gently thrusting his hips forward so he was even deeper in my mouth.

Before he could come I pulled away and stood up to straddle him again. I loved the feeling of his hardness against me, and I rocked my hips against him, so he could feel how wet I was. I moved a hand up to his head, gripping his hair as I leaned in to kiss him. He slid his tongue into my mouth greedily as I continued to slowly rock my hips so just the tip of him slid inside me. He grabbed onto me, trying to pull me down farther but I held his hands away from my body, still moving slowly.

"Poppy," he breathed. "I need to fuck you."

"You will," I whispered, my breath starting to come out in gasps as I rubbed my clit against him, hardly able to control myself from letting him completely fill me.

"Condom," he breathed, kissing the side of my throat.

I couldn't believe I'd almost forgot. I nodded, and Zach rose to his feet, setting me down before he darted toward his bedroom, and returned with a square foil packet.

Once he was ready, I climbed into his lap once again. My intention was to tease him some more, to drive him as wild with desire as he made me, but my body throbbed, and I knew I couldn't hold back for much longer. From the sound of his groaning, I didn't think Zach could either.

Finally, I let go of his hands and he grabbed onto my hips, pulling me down hard so he was fully inside me, even deeper than the first time. I let out a little helpless cry of pleasure at the fullness, rocking my hips to pull him in deeper as his hands remained on my hips, guiding my body down firmly onto his hard cock.

He ran a hand up my neck and into my hair, gripping it in a fist, the other hand reaching down to rub my clit. I was trying not to come too soon, and I let my head fall back, my chest arching forward. Zach leaned forward, taking my breast in his mouth, his tongue expertly doing what his fingers had done a moment before. The sensation of him thrusting inside me while his thumb rubbed my clit and his mouth claimed my breast was too much. I grabbed onto his shoulders, moaning loudly.

"Oh my God," I breathed. My whole body was overcome with pleasure, and I could feel the tension building inside of me. Zach's hand gripped me tighter, and I knew he was close to finishing. I moved my hips faster, my breath coming in gasps, ending in a loud cry, waves of ecstasy swamping all my other senses as I came.

Zach pulled me against him and buried his face in my neck, softly kissing me, then pulled back to look into my eyes. The moment was intense, and we continued to breathe heavily. He was still inside me and I didn't want to move, didn't want the moment to end. I leaned forward and kissed his full lips as he wrapped his arms around me.

"Hold on tight, okay?"

I nodded, moving my hands to his shoulders.

He lifted me up and down over his stiff cock, using my body for his pleasure—and I freaking loved it.

After a few more thrusts, Zach was filling me with his hot semen, making that sexy, satisfied sound again that I was already growing addicted to.

"I didn't think we could top the first time, but that was…" he trailed off.

"Mind-blowing?" I asked.

"I don't think there's a word for how good that was." He pushed my hair from my face, then lifted me off him and led me toward the bedroom. Once we were settled in bed, his arms around me as I snuggled into his side, he turned and smiled at me.

I ran a hand along his chest and snuggled in closer.

"Tell me what you're thinking," he said at last. He'd laid himself bare both in his letter, and then again at his office. And heaven knew we hadn't done much talking tonight.

I guess it was my turn to be brave.

"I'm really glad I came tonight," I whispered.

"Me too."

For once I wasn't thinking about all of the things that could go wrong. We'd have to figure that out eventually, but for now I was just happy to be lying in bed with Zach.

Chapter Twenty-One

Zach

Rolling to my side, I gathered Poppy's warm, sleepy body close to mine. And even though I had yet to open my eyes, a smile spread across my lips. We hadn't done much in the way of talking last night, but what we lacked for in words, I'd written onto her skin, her heart. My flesh had joined with hers, and I knew I'd never be the same. I still didn't know exactly where we stood, but Poppy had stayed all night in my bed, so that had to mean something, right?

"Hey," she said, voice still sleepy.

"Morning." I pressed my lips to her forehead, and Poppy rolled over, so she was facing me.

Even in the light of the morning, she was stunning. She'd packed an overnight bag and had brushed her teeth and washed her face before bed, changing into a little tank top that clung to her curves and a pair of pink boxer shorts. I loved seeing this side to her—the makeup free, wild-haired girl who looked so much younger than her twenty-four years. Like all her defenses were down.

"How did you sleep?" I asked.

Poppy smirked and nudged my erection with her hip. "I kept waking up actually. It felt like we were sleeping with a baseball bat between us."

I chuckled. With Poppy in my bed, my erection hadn't gotten the memo that he could relax. So, despite coming several times last night, he still wasn't sated. Not completely. Probably wouldn't be as long as she was in the same room as me. And I hoped that never changed.

"Sorry about that. Apparently my cock likes you. So do I, Poppy."

She smiled, grinning up at me. "I like you too, Zach. Very much."

"So where do we go from here?" It was a little early to get into conversations of the future, but I saw my opening and I took it.

"Coffee first?" Poppy asked.

I chuckled again, remembering that Poppy loved coffee even more than I did. "Stay right here."

I left the warmth and comfort of my bed and padded barefoot to the kitchen dressed only in the snug boxer briefs I wore to bed. I could feel Poppy's eyes on my ass and broad shoulders as I left the room and I smiled again.

After fixing two large mugs of coffee, I carried them back to bed. Poppy had gathered up all the pillows and was sitting propped up on one side. I handed her a mug and joined her.

"You spoil me. This has all been so unexpected, Zach." She took a sip from her mug, her eyes lingering on mine.

"I want us to be together. This isn't just about sex for me."

"Me either," she whispered.

"But?" I asked, tensing for what I feared she'd say next.

"I want us to be together but the thought of having to hide it from everyone – it sucks, and I don't want to live that way."

"I don't either. I want it all, from the mundane like grocery shopping and doctor's appointments, to the soccer games and dinners in, to making love to you all night. I want to meet your family, and introduce you as my girlfriend. I want it all."

Poppy's eyes were wide and latched onto mine. "I want that too. But what about the rules—the university…"

"I don't know. I don't want to resign from my job any more than you want to resign from the program."

She shook her head. "I don't want it to come to that for either of us."

"I'll figure it out, Poppy. I'll fix this. Trust me?"

"I shouldn't, but I do."

I set my mug on the bedside table, and took Poppy's and placed it next to mine. "Come here." Gathering her close, I peppered her lips and throat with kisses.

"Are you always this … excited?" She made a point of nudging her hip against my erection and I couldn't help but chuckle.

"With you half-naked in my bed? Yes."

"Will I get extra credit for helping you take care of this?"

"Y-yes," I choked out, excitedly, but rather inarticulately.

She giggled. "Then let me see what I can do."

Poppy removed her tank top and shorts, and then pushed my boxer briefs down so my heavy cock sprang free and rested on my belly, already leaking precum.

If Poppy was going to be in my life, I'd have to have a long talk with my cock—there was no need to be so greedy and immature.

Lifting one leg in a way she made look elegant, Poppy came to rest in my lap—straddling me. I placed my hands on her hips and guided her toward my waiting cock.

"Condom?" I breathed when she was nestled right there—her warm, wet heat licking the head of my cock.

She shook her head, offering me a coy smile. "I'm on birth control. And I trust you."

Knowing that she was sharing this was me—the intimacy of fucking bare—which was only reserved for serious monogamous relationships and people you loved and trust, it made my heart clench inside my chest.

"I trust you too," I said, voice husky.

And if something happened and we accidentally gave Connor a little brother or sister, I had to admit, I didn't hate the idea of that, not one single bit in fact.

Helping support her weight above me, I used my grasp on Poppy's hips to lower her down onto me. She tossed her head back and let out a soft cry.

"Holy hell, Zach."

"You look so beautiful riding me," I murmured, pressing a kiss to her parted lips.

Together, we found our rhythm, moving as one while the morning sun bathed us in her warmth.

And as for what would happen next? I would just have to wait and see.

Chapter Twenty-Two

Poppy

I checked my phone anxiously as I stepped out of my car. Zach said he'd take care of things, but if he had he was leaving me in the dark. Then, the director of the program, Lewis Clybourne, had emailed me this morning asking me to meet before class. I'd texted Zach, hoping he had some insight as to what was going on, but I hadn't heard back. Was it possible Dr. Clybourne had found out about me and Zach? But how? We'd been discreet, as far as I knew.

Briefly I wondered if someone could have overheard us in Zach's office the other day, when things had turned heated. I bit my nail, a bad habit I'd mostly kicked but that still came out when I was particularly nervous. Suddenly this whole situation seemed like a huge mistake.

My heart pounded as I approached Clybourne's door. When he opened it, Zach was already seated inside. My mouth dropped open in shock. What was he doing here?

"Come in, Poppy." Dr. Clybourne smiled, his eyes crinkling in the corners.

I gathered myself and smiled back nervously, taking a seat uncertainly next to Zach. I wanted to catch his eye, hoping he could silently convey what was going on, but Clybourne started talking before I had the chance.

"So, you're probably wondering why you're here." He shut the door and returned to his desk to take a seat.

"Is everything okay?" I asked, trying not to let worry creep into my voice. I didn't know how much he knew, and I didn't want to give anything away.

"Things have taken an interesting turn, but yes, I think it will be," he said kindly. "I just wanted to have this meeting to keep everyone on the same page." He looked at me over his black-framed glasses. "Zach has requested that we switch you to a new adviser."

My mouth dropped open again and I quickly closed it. I looked in Zach's direction. He looked back at me, but his face was impassive. What was happening?

"Normally we'd never do this, but Zach came forward about your relationship and we felt it would be in everyone's best interest if we found you a new adviser," he continued. "We think you have a great talent and we want to make sure you have an adviser who can critique your work and give you unbiased feedback."

I forced myself to smile and nod, relief washing over me. I couldn't believe it. He was actually okay with our relationship?

"That sounds … great. Thank you so much."

"Of course." He stood up, signaling the end of the meeting. "And if you ever have any questions, just let me know."

I stood, my legs still slightly numb, and walked out of his office with Zach. I didn't say anything as we walked toward his office, not wanting to be overheard. After we were safely inside, I let out a big sigh of relief.

"I can't believe you told him about us," I said, gaping. I laughed, thinking about how nervous I'd been walking in. "I was freaking out when I saw his email requesting the meeting."

Zach smiled apologetically, running his hands along my arms. "I'm sorry about that. I was caught up in meetings and didn't get your text. I would have given you a heads-up, but I had no idea he'd want to meet with us both."

"I'm just glad he wasn't upset. Weren't you afraid they'd fire you?"

He ran a hand through his hair, taking a seat behind his desk and motioning me toward the chair in front of him "Honestly, a little. But I just told him the truth. That we hadn't expected this to happen but after spending so much time together we developed feelings. And I wasn't just saying it, I really think you should be with an adviser who is objective about your work."

"I can't believe he took it so well." I was still in a state of disbelief.

He winked. "I'd done my research. I'm not a professor, not someone grading your work—as administrative staff, the guidelines are more gray. And I consulted a friend of mine. He said it's better to come forward and get ahead of it before you're discovered."

I raised an eyebrow. "I almost can't believe it. So we're good?"

He laughed. "Yes, Poppy. We're good. We have some other things to figure out between us, but we won't have to hide from the university."

Leaning over his desk, I placed my hand in his.

"Thank you."

Zach gave my hand a squeeze, his fingertips lightly rubbing the back of my hand. "You were worth the risk."

I glanced at my watch and stood up quickly. "Shit, I should probably get to class. I'm going to be late."

"Wait." Zach got up and walked over to me, pulling me against him. His soft lips met mine, and my body melted against him as he kissed me. I automatically put my hands on his chest, gripping his shirt.

I pushed back, giving him a little shove on the chest. "I have to go to class," I said breathily.

He smirked. "I know."

"Maybe we can continue this tonight, at my place?" I grinned. "Connor was practically begging to see you again."

Zach nodded, smiling, "I've missed that guy. It's a date."

As I was leaving his office, I gave Zach another quick kiss goodbye. When I turned to leave, I saw Kody and Jodee had rounded the corner on their way to class. They must have seen the kiss, because their mouths were hanging open, and they'd stopped dead in their tracks.

Kody put a hand up. "Hold on. What is this?"

I shrugged, hoping he'd drop it. I felt my face get hot. I had never been one for public displays of affection, especially with my ex-adviser.

"So, this is happening now?" Jodee asked hopefully, looking back and forth between us.

Zach and I exchanged looks.

"It's happening." I grinned.

"Thank God." Kody rolled his eyes. "I was about to take matters into my own hands if your little stand-off didn't end soon." Then Kody sauntered over to Zach and looked him up and down. "Just know one thing. You won't get a second chance with me."

Zach laughed. "Sorry, man. It was a tempting offer, but I had to go with Poppy in the end."

"We should probably get to class," I said, ushering them along, not wanting to subject Zach to any more of their antics.

"I'll call you later," he called out as we headed down the hall.

I could feel Kody and Jodee practically bursting with things to say as we walked away. As soon as we rounded the corner, they both grabbed my arms.

"Oh my God," Jodee exclaimed. "This is crazy."

"Lucky bitch, now you have an adorable kid *and* a hot boyfriend?" Kody pouted.

"You can borrow my adorable kid whenever you want." I laughed. "I'd say the same about my hot boyfriend, but I'm not sure he'd be happy about it."

Kody smiled, looping an arm through mine as we headed to class. "I'll settle for the kid."

* * *

That night, I was still riding the high of the day when I walked in the front door.

"Mom, look." Connor came running into the hallway and tugged my arm, pulling me toward the living room.

My mom had been watching him while I was in class, and she was crouched on the floor, putting down the last pieces of a puzzle.

"Look at the puzzle I'm doing." Connor was still holding onto my arm, pulling me toward the floor so I could get a better look. Of course, it was astronaut themed. It was halfway finished, so I could only see part of a spaceship travelling through the stars.

"You did this all by yourself?"

"Grandma helped." He grinned.

"This is amazing," I said, pulling him in for a hug. "We can finish it later tonight."

My mom was looking me up and down, assessing me with a smile on her face.

"What?" I asked. I cursed myself for how defensive I sounded. She would see right through that.

"Nothing." She shrugged. "You're just practically glowing right now. Good day at school?" She was smirking at me, and I knew she knew about Zach. I had no idea how, but she always knew these kinds of things.

Before I could respond my phone buzzed. It was Zach, letting me know he'd be over soon. When I looked back up my mom was still watching me, and I realized I'd been grinning at my phone.

"Can you stop?" I asked, laughing. "I'm just in a good mood. Is that so hard to believe?"

"Of course not, honey." She smiled, pulling on her coat and picking up her purse. As I hugged her goodbye, she whispered in my ear, "Say hi to Zach for me."

"Mom," I exclaimed, half laughing half embarrassed at how easily she'd figured me out.

I was still grinning to myself as I watched her pull out of the driveway. I sat on the couch and Connor knelt back on the floor, trying to fit the next piece into the puzzle. I couldn't wait to see the look on his face when Zach walked in the door.

I was still reeling, not only from everything that had happened that day, but from everything that had happened during these past few months. What had started out as a stupid plan to have a fake boyfriend for one night had somehow turned into a real relationship. And not only did I now have the world's greatest boyfriend, I could focus on school more seriously with an adviser who I wasn't constantly imagining naked. Connor would have an amazing male role model who he adored and who adored him back. Now that everything had worked out, it seemed crazy that I'd ever thought this was so complicated. In fact, being with Zach made everything seem so much easier.

I glanced at the time before kneeling next to Connor to help with the puzzle. Zach would be on his way over soon. My phone buzzed again. It was Zach saying that he was going to make dinner for me and Connor, and I couldn't think of a better way to end my day.

Chapter Twenty-Three

Zach

I wanted to pretend I wasn't nervous about this, but fuck—I just was.

Poppy and I had been dating for six months, and piece by piece, I'd torn down all her walls, shown her day by day that I was going to be there for her and Connor, that I wasn't going to get scared off or disappear on her like the men in her past. All of the grand declarations and love poems in the world wouldn't have proven my allegiance. Poppy was a take-action kind of girl, and so the only way to convince her I would be here, was to show her day by day.

I'd met her parents, and she'd met mine, and now the next step was asking her and Connor to move in with me. I wasn't quite sure how Poppy would react, but I knew I was ready. The idea of waking up to her each morning and sharing our bedtime routine together made my inside go all fucking melty. I was crazy about this girl, and I knew the future I wanted. Since Poppy's lease was up, I needed to ask now, or be stuck waiting another year—an idea that did not appeal to me. I had a feeling she might protest the idea of living together, probably something about Connor needing stability as the reason. But I wasn't going to let her use him as a buffer for doing things that scared her. Not when Connor and I were as thick as thieves. Which was why I hatched my plan today.

"Which one do you think she'd like best, buddy?" I leaned down closer to Connor where he peered wide-eyed into the glass jewelry counter with all of its sparkling earrings, tennis bracelets, and rings.

The saleslady helping us offered a shy smile as she watched us.

Tomorrow was Poppy's twenty-fifth birthday, and she and Connor were coming over for dinner to celebrate. So far, we'd hit the bakery and florist, where Connor got to select a cake and flowers for her and now we were at the jewelry store where it was my turn to spoil her.

Poppy was at home, finishing her poetry collection that would be turned in to Dr. Chan for her final. I was already daydreaming of all the adventures we could take Connor on this summer with both Poppy and Connor out of school…hiking in the mountains, camping, to the old drive-in movie theater I loved when I was a kid.

"What about this one?" Connor asked, pointing at a diamond solitaire in white gold. The kid had damn good taste. It had to be at least two karats.

The saleslady reached inside the cabinet and pulled out the ring. "This is actually more of an engagement ring," she clarified.

"You know, for when two people want to get married," I added, unsure if Connor knew what it meant to get engaged.

His eyes widened and swung over to mine. "You mean, you and my mom ...?"

I sank to my knees so we were eye-level, where we could talk, man-to man. "I love your mom. And I love you too, Connor. And even though I would love to one day marry her, I wouldn't do anything that you weren't ready for."

He thought it over, his eyes narrowing and wandering over the store as he thought. "So you'd be like my dad."

I nodded. "I would be honored."

"And we'd all live together?"

I nodded again. "Yeah."

He continued thinking, his nose scrunching. "Your house or ours?"

"Well, if you guys were okay with it, I was thinking my house."

"Your backyard is pretty awesome." He grinned, flashing his smile that was now sans two front teeth.

"That it is." I almost mentioned that we could build the tree house we'd drawn up, before stopping myself. I didn't want him agreeing to this whole plan because I'd bribed him into it. And the truth was, I'd build that tree house for him whether or not they moved in.

Connor's mouth curved into a huge smile before he turned to look at the saleslady. "We'll take it."

I probably should have asked her to see the price, but I was so in shock, so ridiculously fucking happy that I merely nodded at her.

Then I pulled Connor into a huge hug. "What do you think your mom will say?" Moment of truth. I held my breath while I waited for him to answer.

"Oh, she'll cry for sure." He grinned.

* * *

Later that night, I'd just finished cleaning the dinner dishes while Poppy and Connor moved in to the living room to get more comfortable.

Then I carried a slice of chocolate cake with a single candle lit toward them. Poppy's face lit up in a smile and Connor began singing Happy Birthday, a little off-key, but adorably.

"Make a wish," I encouraged, setting the plate down on the coffee table in front of her.

"But I have everything I could ever need right here." She reached out and squeezed my hand, her other resting on Connor's back as he peered down at the cake like it held magical power.

"Not everything, Mom. Me and Zach got you ..."

I shook my head. "I'll ask her later, buddy."

I'd debated with myself about giving her the ring now, but didn't want Connor's obvious excitement to play into her decision. I needed to know that she wanted me—regardless of anything else. Which meant I needed to propose in private.

Connor looked disappointed, but nodded his understanding.

Poppy's eyebrows drew together as she studied us, but then I nudged her, and she leaned over her cake and blew out the candle.

After cake, champagne for the grownups, and a bubble bath for Connor, I tucked him into the guest room. I'd gotten new sheets just for him—printed with space scenes and faraway galaxies and a rocket-shaped night-light too.

It was only the second time I'd gotten Poppy to agree to a sleepover, and the first was due to a massive snowstorm this past winter that made driving downright treacherous. Tonight was a big deal on its own, but Poppy had no idea about the ring that was burning a hole in my pocket.

I found Poppy in the kitchen pouring us each a second glass of champagne.

"Happy Birthday, Poppy." I pressed a kiss to her mouth and accepted the champagne flute.

"Thank you, Zach. It's been perfect."

"You're finally catching up to me." I'd turned thirty a couple of months ago and Poppy liked pointing out that she was dating an old man.

"I don't think that's how it works." She chuckled and followed me into the living room where we cuddled on the couch and sipped our champagne.

A little voice inside my head pointed out that maybe I was rushing this, that even if I was ready, even if Connor was amenable to the idea, Poppy might not be ready. We'd only been dating six months after all, but when you knew, you just knew. I just hoped we were on the same page.

"What did you have to ask me?" Poppy asked, gazing thoughtfully at me where I sat next to her.

Gathering my courage, I set my glass down on the table.

Rising to my feet, I felt the weight of Poppy's stare as I shoved one hand into my jeans pocket and withdrew the tiny symbol of my love and devotion.

Suddenly standing before her, I wished I'd planned something more romantic, wished I'd written something magical for her. I felt woefully unprepared, and while I'd wanted this to be simple and sincere, I questioned if I'd fucked this up before I even started.

But then I dropped to both knees to kneel before her, and Poppy brought her fingertips to her lips, her expression filled with wonderment.

I opened my palm and set the ring on her legging-covered knee.

"Zach...?" Her tone was filled with surprise, and she sat up straighter, although carefully so as to not disturb the ring where it balanced.

"From that first moment you approached me at the party, you've owned a piece of my heart. You're brilliant and funny and so goddamn beautiful, Poppy. I've fallen in love with you and I'm ready to pledge my forever to you. If you'll have me."

"But what about Connor ... it's so much to ask, Zach."

I shook my head. "It's not too much to ask. I get so much in return—from both of you. You've both brought meaning into my life, a purpose, and I've known I've wanted this, wanted you, wanted forever, from the moment I saw you."

A single tear slipped down her cheek as she watched

me.

"And I kind of already cleared it with Connor, anyway. He's cool with it." I couldn't help but smirk.

At this Poppy laughed as the tears fell down her cheeks…and it was the best sound I'd ever heard in the entire world.

"Yes, Zach. Yes!" I grabbed the ring and slid it onto her finger as she all but leaped into my arms.

The ring looked perfect on her slender finger, the sparkly diamond picking up the light so brilliantly.

"You're stuck with me now."

"Forever," she murmured, bringing her lips to mine.

We heard a small shout of approval come from the guest bedroom and pulled apart.

I chuckled. "I think our cheering section approves."

Epilogue

Zach

"I think I fudged this eggnog up. It has the consistency of semen," my mother chuckled under her breath.

Poppy winked at her. "I'll try some."

This sent them both into a fit of giggles, and I took it as my cue to exit the kitchen.

Since my mother had put me in charge of setting the table, I busied myself with placemats and folding cloth napkins—probably a little more forcefully than necessary.

Poppy followed me, placing one hand over mine. "Relax, babe. She's just being silly."

My gaze cut over toward Connor who was stringing lights on my mother's dusty old artificial tree in the family room.

"I just don't want Connor to overhear anything he shouldn't. I want him to be a kid for as long as he can."

Poppy smiled at me and took my hand. "He will be. And he can't hear us. That movie is outrageously loud."

I glanced at the TV where the classic Grinch film was playing and nodded. "Yeah, I guess so."

"Was she like this when you were little?" Poppy asked.

I shook my head. "No, she's gotten dirtier as she's gotten older."

"So, I wonder if that's a genetic thing and I have *that* to look forward to." Poppy winked at me, and lifted up on her toes to press a kiss to my lips.

I shook my head and rested a hand on her growing belly. "I'm sorry I'm a grouch. I love you."

"I love you too. Now go get a beer or something— you don't really have to abstain just because I do. That's silly."

I shook my head. "No, I'm fine. It's just …" I let out a sigh, my eyes wandering over to where my mother and father cooked side by side in the kitchen. Her mashing potatoes, him slicing the roast.

I hadn't spent a Christmas Eve with both of my parents since I was three years old.

"It's really throwing you off seeing them together,

isn't it?"

I nodded, reluctant to admit that to her.

My parents hadn't had a relationship at all after their divorce, not even any of that brave new-world stuff people spoke about like co-parenting or joint family vacations. But since being reunited for the first time in decades at mine and Poppy's wedding last spring, slowly but surely, they had become friends.

"It's just … weird, isn't it?"

Every time they shared a knowing smile, or a laugh, I couldn't help but be caught off guard, wondering what alternate universe I'd stumbled into. But each time my mom made a dirty joke about the turkey's breasts, or my dad offered to lend her a hand with something, it was the strangest feeling. I never imagined I'd spend time with them in the same room again—a thought that while depressing, I'd resigned myself too. So to see them laughing and getting along? It was astonishing. I doubted anything romantic would ever develop between them ever again, but they were each getting older, and hell, everyone could use a good friend, a companion, no matter what your age. I guess I was the only one left to get on board with this arrangement.

Poppy smiled at me again like she knew something I didn't. "I don't know, I think it's nice."

"Maybe I will have that beer. Just one."

"Good idea, honey," Poppy encouraged, pressing another kiss to my lips.

I rubbed my hand along the firm bump of her stomach, marveling at how round it had become. I loved seeing her like this, full of my child. Our child. "Are you feeling okay? Not too tired?"

She told me she'd been so sick with Connor, but with this baby, she felt great—tons of energy, healthy, and most of all happy. And I was too. I was over the fucking moon. It'd be just over a year since I'd first met Poppy and my life had changed dramatically.

She shook her head. "I feel fine. But I don't want to stay too late, because we've still got some wrapping to do when we get home." She whispered that last part.

I shook my head. "We won't stay late, but I finished the wrapping while you took a shower this afternoon."

This earned me another kiss, and then together, we strode back into the kitchen where Poppy fetched me a bottle of beer from the fridge and handed it to me without a word.

Over dinner, and then after way too much pie, my mother continued to be endearingly inappropriate, keeping us all entertained.

"So, Connor, what are you most excited about with the new baby coming?" my dad asked.

I gazed over at the amazing young man I had adopted as my own shortly after Poppy and I were married. He made me so proud on a daily basis. The way he'd accepted me into their lives, accepted my marriage to his mother, and now his excitement over the baby, it was all so incredible.

Connor thought about it for a minute, and I could see his wheels were turning. He was really processing the question and what his answer might be. "For a long time it was just me and my mom. And then Zach came, and it's been super fun. I guess what I'm most excited about is having another person in the family to love. I used to beg her for a dog, and she always said no. But I realize now that having a family is way better than a dog."

A lump formed in my throat, and Poppy's hand

found mine beneath the table.

"Amen to that, sweetheart," my mother said, reaching over to give Connor's shoulder a squeeze. "Come on, Connor. Let's pack you up a slice of pie to take home for breakfast." My mom winked at him conspiratorially.

"I'll clean up," dad said waving us away.

"Come here, Poppy. There's something I want to show you." I rose from the table, and helped her out of her chair. Poppy followed me back to the bedroom that used to be mine when I was a little boy.

"Your old room?" she asked. "I've already seen it."

I closed the door behind us. "No. Not my old room. Take a seat."

Poppy shot me a questioning glare, but sat down on my old twin-sized mattress covered with a patchwork quilt.

I walked closer, stopping to stand in front of her and pulled a folded envelope from my pocket. It was just a simple sheet of paper inside, but damn if it hasn't been burning a hole in my pocket all night. Maybe that's why my mother irritated me so badly earlier. It wasn't my parents' strange new relationship that was bothering me— it was keeping a secret from Poppy that was weighing on me. I swallowed down a sudden wave of nerves.

"I made you a promise the night I proposed. And then I vowed those promises before God, and our families the day of our wedding."

"Zach?" Poppy asked, eyebrows lifting in confusion.

I took a deep breath, unfolding the envelope in my hands. "I vowed to you that I would always love, cherish, and provide for you and our children."

Poppy licked her lips, her gaze jumping between my eyes and the paper in my hands.

"I work every day to make sure you feel loved and cherished. And as for providing … I know my salary at the university isn't much …"

"That's not true. It's great, Zach. The benefits alone are…"

"But I want more for you. For us." We had what we needed, but we didn't have money for fancy vacations, or hell, even stashing away in savings.

She nodded, eyes still filled with questions.

"This." I pulled the sheet of paper from the envelope it had rested inside of for the last three days. "Is part of that future."

Poppy took the envelope from my hands, and slowly opened it. Her eyes scanned the page in an almost desperate attempt to understand.

"I don't … I don't understand. They want to publish your book?"

"Our book, Poppy. They're offering me, offering us …" I pointed at the number two paragraphs down.

"Three hundred thousand dollars?" Poppy's voice was breathless as she squinted at me.

I nodded. "For our story."

I'd gone on submission with my book last fall, and while I had faith in my work, an offer like this was almost unheard of. Especially on a debut novel. My agent had asked for some changes, she wanted the book to be book-club friendly and that meant some major rewrites, including making the book fiction and taking a few creative liberties, but it was still my story, still Poppy's story. It was our love affair and her single motherhood and chasing our dreams, all the good and bad times spelled out for the world to see.

"Oh my God, Zach." Tears welled in her eyes and spilled over, silently rolling down her cheeks as she stared at me, open-mouthed and amazed.

The chance to see my work in bookstores was incredible. The money was an aside. But it meant Poppy could stay home with the baby if she wanted to. At least for the first year. She'd graduate this spring. Right around the time the baby was due. I loved that she'd be under no pressure to take on more hours at her marketing job or settle for something less than she was worth.

"I know." I kissed her and hugged her.

When she squeezed me tight, the bump between us was a reminder of all that was good in the world.

"Why didn't you tell me? What didn't you tell everyone at dinner?"

I shook my head, pulling her to her feet and holding her close. "I wanted to save it. Wanted it to be a surprise. A Christmas surprise."

Her hand came to rest on her belly, the other on my

cheek. "I love you so much. And I am so immensely proud of you."

"They want to keep the title as xo, Zach." That bit of information made me incredibly happy, and I could tell it had the same effect on Poppy as fresh tears blurred her eyes.

"You did it, Zach."

"We did."

A little while later, we led a protesting little boy out of his grandma's house with the promise that he could open just one gift when we got home.

After the gift was opened and Christmas cookies were eaten, finally, finally, Connor was in bed and I was alone with Poppy.

"Oh my God, did you see how cute he looked in those footie pajamas?" she asked as we headed down the hall to our own bedroom, now dead tired.

I nodded. "I'm glad you liked them. There's a pair for you under the tree, too."

This earned me one of her laughs, that I never seemed to tire of. "You found them in maternity sizing?"

"Heck no. They're going to be skin-tight on you. It'll be amazing."

Closing our bedroom door behind us, she turned to face me and leveled me with a pointed stare. "You're just gross, old man."

"There's nothing gross about your body. I love all the changes." My hands found her hips, now fuller, and I tugged her closer, close enough to feel the hard ridge in my jeans.

"Seriously? The thought of me in footie pajamas—that gets you hard?"

I couldn't help the chuckle that tumbled from my lips. "Are you not in the mood?"

Most days she was still up for it—but I was waiting for her libido to change, or just for her to tire of being newlyweds, but so far, our passion hadn't cooled.

"I didn't say that." Placing her palm against my denim-covered erection, Poppy let out a soft noise—sort of a happy sigh that made my insides quiver. "Does my husband need some attention?"

I pressed my lips to hers. "Maybe … if you're up for it."

"I think we need to properly celebrate that massive publishing contract. Don't you?" Poppy lifted her arms, allowing me to pull her sweater off over her head.

"I won't protest that. What did you have in mind?"

Poppy unlatched my belt, and worked her hand inside my jeans, stroking the length of my cock with her soft, delicate hand. "Want you."

The swell of her ample cleavage jiggled as she worked her hand up and down.

"Fuck that feels good."

Poppy let out another of those toe-curling noises.

In about three seconds flat, I had her stripped naked and on the bed next to me. She was only six months along, but already we'd gotten creative with our lovemaking. I knew from here on out, finding a position that made Poppy feel both comfortable and sexy would keep me on my toes. Tonight it seemed I had succeeded. With us laying side by side, I lifted her top leg and placed it over my hip so I could align myself with her.

"Is this okay?" I asked, voice breathless.

"Yes. Please," she whispered. "I want you."

With her legs spread before me, I had the perfect access to stroke her clit and suck and kiss her breasts as I thrust inside, slowly but deeply.

We moved together, perfectly in sync until we both came in a hot, sticky rush.

Then I lovingly cleaned up my glowing bride and covered us in our down comforter.

This was my perfection. A warm, sleepy Poppy in my arms and our first Christmas morning to enjoy with our son tomorrow.

"I have one last surprise for you," I whispered in the dark.

"There's more? What is it?" Poppy asked.

I lifted her hand and placed her fingers over my heart.

She pushed the blankets aside and squinted in the dimly lit room, trying to make out the script. It was a new tattoo, her name—written in her own script, inked right over my heart.

"How did you get this? When?"

I swallowed down a sudden wave of emotion. When

the artist had finished, and I saw her tidy writing scrawled across my skin, knowing it would be there for all of eternity, I'd felt moved—but now seeing it again through Poppy's eyes, it was almost just as powerful.

"I took a piece of paper you had signed for school with me, and the artist re-created it."

"Oh Zach. This is …"

"Do you like it?"

She nodded slowly, eyes huge. "I love you so much."

"I love you too, Poppy."

The truth was, I fell more in love with her with each passing day.

Our story wasn't yet complete, but with each new chapter we wrote, I found that I never wanted it to end.

Up Next

Baby Daddy (a standalone romantic comedy)

We met in a trapped elevator.

Emmett was on his way to work, sophisticated and handsome in his tailored suit and tie.

I was on my way to the sperm bank. *Awkward, right?*

At thirty-five, my life hadn't taken the path I thought it would and I was tired of waiting—I wanted a baby. And I was ready to take matters into my own hands to make it happen.

After our ill-fated elevator encounter, Emmett insisted on taking me to dinner—he also insisted on something else—that I ditch my plan involving a turkey baster and let him do the job. He would be my baby daddy. He was a wealthy and powerful CEO with little interest in diapers or playdates. And since he didn't want kids, I'd be on my own once his bun was in my oven, free to go my own way.

But once his baby was inside me, it was like a switch had been flipped, and I got a whole lot more than I ever bargained for.

Acknowledgements

A big thank you to my editing team on this novel. First to Elaine York and Becca Hensley for the editing you did that helped to flesh out the story so perfectly, and to Caitlyn Alario thank you for polishing my words, and finally to Virginia Tesi Carey for your eagle-eyes, thank you for pouring over this with a fine-toothed comb and making sure it was perfect (or damn near!).

Thank you to my fabulous publicist and right hand in all the things, Dani—you rock my world. And a giant thank you to my whole team—Ashley and Alyssa, I don't even want to imagine a world without you. Thank you for keeping this busy mama sane.

To my dear, sweet husband for being my everything, my reason, and for introducing me to Warm Cookie Wednesday.

And last, but certainly not least—thank you to my readers. You guys are everything. I would love to hear your thoughts on xo, Zach. Please leave a review at your favorite retailer, and be sure to email me your thoughts too. I love hearing from you.

kendall@kendallryanbooks.com.

Get a Free Book

Did you know that just for signing up for my mailing list, I'll send you a copy of my recent bestselling title, Dirty Little Secret? What are you waiting for – it's book one in a brand-new series and features not one, but two hot demanding alpha males!

Get your copy here:

www.forbiddendesiresseries.com